STAR WARS

ROGUE ONE ™

A JUNIOR NOVEL

WRITTEN BY MATT FORBECK

BASED ON THE STORY BY JOHN KNOLL AND GARY WHITTA
AND THE SCREENPLAY BY CHRIS WEITZ AND TONY GILROY

EGMONT

EGMONT

We bring stories to life

First published in Great Britain 2017
by Egmont UK Limited, The Yellow Building,
1 Nicholas Road, London W11 4AN

© & ™ 2017 Lucasfilm Ltd.

ISBN 978 1 4052 8568 1
66810/1

Printed in UK

A long time ago in a galaxy far,
far away. . . .

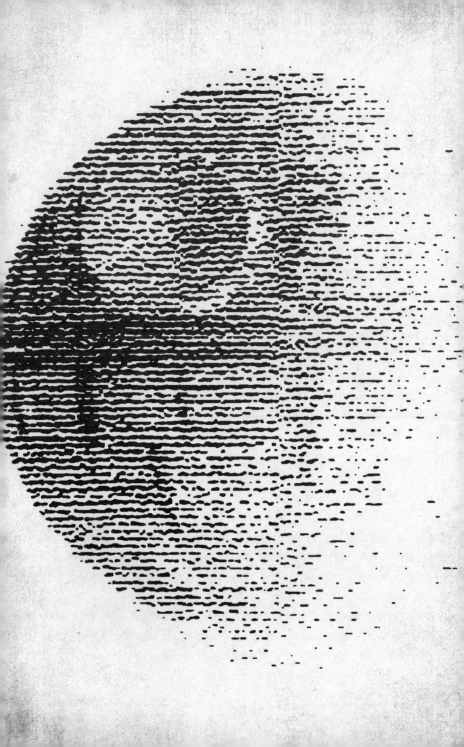

CHAPTER 1

JYN ERSO REMEMBERED the exact day the Empire destroyed her life. She was only eight years old, and she and her parents—Galen and Lyra—were living on Lah'mu, a backwater planet far from the luxurious home they'd once known on the Imperial capital world, Coruscant.

Jyn spotted the Imperial shuttle scudding through the sky and knew it meant trouble. She raced home from where she'd been playing alone in the thick lush grass to warn her parents, but they were already packing.

"Jyn," her father told her, "gather your things. It's time."

They'd drilled countless times for this. While Jyn followed Galen's orders, Lyra activated the family's comm unit. "Saw," she said. "It's happened. He's come for us."

Before Lyra took Jyn from their home, Galen gave his daughter one last kiss.

"I love you, Stardust," he said.

"I love you, too, Papa."

The shuttle landed outside, and six death troopers emerged in their shiny black armor, along with an Imperial officer in a white uniform and cape. Jyn recognized him. He had worked with her father back on Coruscant. His name was Orson Krennic.

Lyra took her by the arm and led her through the back door while her father went to greet their visitors. Once they were out of sight, Lyra took off her necklace and put it on Jyn. The kyber crystal pendant sparkled in the light.

"You know where to go, don't you?" Lyra asked.

Jyn nodded.

"Trust the Force," Lyra said as she hugged her daughter, and somehow Jyn knew she meant good-bye.

Despite her orders to run and hide, Jyn refused to leave her parents behind. She covertly trailed her mother back to the house and watched as her father confronted Krennic.

"What is it you want?" Galen demanded.

"The work has stalled," Krennic said. "I need you to come back."

"I won't do it."

"We were on the verge of greatness. We were this close to providing peace. Security for the galaxy."

"You're confusing peace with terror. You lied about what we were building. You wanted to kill people."

Krennic shrugged. "You have to start somewhere."

Lyra stepped forward then. Mystified why she would show herself—against the plan they'd drilled—Jyn watched in horror. When the death troopers spotted Lyra, they turned their weapons on her, but Krennic ordered them to hold their fire.

That's when Lyra revealed the blaster she was carrying and leveled it at Krennic.

"You're not taking him," she said.

"Of course not." Krennic smiled. "I'm taking you all. You, your child. You'll all live in comfort."

"As hostages," Lyra said.

"As 'heroes of the Empire.'"

Lyra refused to lower her weapon. "You'll never win," she said.

Krennic came to a decision. "Do it," he ordered the death troopers.

8

The elite Imperial soldiers shot Lyra down, but not before she got off a shot of her own, which struck Krennic in the shoulder. Jyn knew, though, that the Imperial officer would recover. Her mother never would.

Galen caught Lyra as she fell. Her weight and his grief brought him to his knees.

"They have a child," Krennic said to the death troopers, through teeth gritted in pain. "Find it."

Jyn fled.

She knew where to go, just like they'd done in their drills. But she didn't know if she could get there before the death troopers found her.

She ran without looking back. She reached a cave in the rocky hills behind her house, and she dashed into it. There she lifted a concealed hatch and slipped through, closing it behind her.

She stayed there, gazing out at the daylight through a crack in the hatch. When the death troopers hunting for her came close, she held her breath and went as still as a statue. When they finally passed by, she crept deeper into her hidey-hole and waited, just as she'd been told.

She remained there for hours, alone. She smelled smoke in the air, from a fire she later learned was consuming her home. At one point, she thought she heard the shuttle leave, but she knew that she was to stay put until one of her parents came for her.

But what if that never happened? If her mother was already dead and the death troopers had taken her father, no one would ever come for her. She would be on her own.

She huddled in the dark as night fell, terrified and unsure what to do. A storm came raging through, and she startled at the sound of thunder.

She lit a lantern and tried to keep her spirits up. Eventually, she would have to defy her parents' orders, but when? Not until the storm had passed, for sure.

Before that happened, though, she heard a noise above and froze. This was not thunder but footsteps, coming closer. Someone had entered the cave.

A moment later, the hatch opened, and the man Lyra had been talking to on the comm unit stared down at Jyn. Saw Gerrera.

"Come, my child," he said as he offered her his hand. "We have a long ride ahead of us."

That had been many years before. A lot of things had happened since then. More things than Jyn cared to count. They'd all added up to put her where she was now: rotting away in an Imperial prison and wondering how she'd fought so hard and long just to wind up there.

CHAPTER 2

CASSIAN ANDOR had done a lot of horrible things as a member of the Rebel Alliance, all in the name of helping put an end to the Galactic Empire. Rather than tossing him in prison for those crimes, his Alliance commanders had promoted him to the rank of captain and given him even more impossible missions. He sometimes wondered if they secretly wanted him to fail so they could wash their hands of him, but he remained too determined to give in to such wishes.

For his latest assignment, they'd sent him to the Ring of Kafrene, a pair of gigantic asteroids that spun in tandem through a field of smaller rocks floating in space. Long before, someone had joined them and used them to establish the scummiest trading post in that horrible part of the galaxy. There, Cassian met a spy named Tivik, who supposedly had some explosive news the Alliance needed from Jedha, an ancient place known for worship of the Force.

They met in a dead-end alley. Every bit of Tivik twitched, except for his bad arm, which hung limp at his side. He seemed so nervous that Cassian wondered if he might bolt before he started talking, but once he began, everything spilled out.

"An Imperial pilot—one of the cargo drivers—he defected yesterday," Tivik reported. "He's telling people they're making a weapon. The kyber crystals? That's what they're for. He brought a message. He's got proof."

Suspicious, Cassian squared off against the man. "What kind of weapon?"

Tivik glanced around, searching for a way out. "Look, I have to go."

Cassian grabbed him. *"What kind of weapon?"*

"A planet killer." Tivik cringed beneath Cassian's glare. "That's what he called it."

Tivik went on to explain that Galen Erso—an old friend of Saw Gerrera's—had sent the pilot. Tivik was angry about the Alliance and how little it had done to help Saw in his fight.

"Saw's right! You guys keep talking and stalling and dealing, and we're on fumes out there! There's spies everywhere. . . ."

Tivik trailed off as he spotted a pair of stormtroopers entering the alley. They walked toward Cassian and Tivik, demanding to see their scandocs.

Cassian wasn't about to let anyone take him in. He reached into his pocket, but instead of producing identification, he grabbed his silenced blaster and used it to put a hole straight through each of the stormtroopers.

Tivik recoiled in horror. "No! What have you done?"

A third stormtrooper appeared at the far end of the alley. Rather than charge in to be shot, he called for backup. "Troopers down. Section nine."

Cassian scanned the alley for a means of escape and spotted some easy handholds he could use to climb out. With Tivik's damaged arm, though, he'd never make it.

Cassian couldn't leave him there to be captured. The man would crack for sure, and if he told the Empire what he knew . . .

Cassian had no choice. He leveled his blaster and shot Tivik dead. The stormtrooper stood there, stunned, and watched the man fall.

Cassian took advantage of that moment to throw himself against the nearest wall and start climbing. He had to move fast, or he'd have to shoot himself, too.

CHAPTER 3

JYN HAD resigned herself to prison. After running from place to place for so long, it was something of a relief to finally be able to stop.

Besides, as far as she could see, there was no way out of this one, at least not on her own. Not yet.

She was on a work detail, riding with a few other hard cases to a site where they'd be set to breaking rocks or shoveling garbage out of a compactor—whatever nasty work the Empire needed done. They had three stormtroopers in the back of their ride to guard just five prisoners, which seemed like over-kill, but Jyn didn't care to tell the Imperial Prison Service how to do its job.

The transport ground to a halt, and a moment later, a magnetic grenade blew the front door open. Blaster fire took down the three troopers fast, and an armed man stormed in shouting for Liana Hallik.

Jyn recognized the name. It was the one she'd been using when she was arrested. Still, she remained quiet.

It didn't matter. The next soldier who came through the door recognized her.

"You want to get out of here?" the first one said.

Jyn gave him a hesitant nod, and a third soldier moved up and removed her shackles. One of her fellow prisoners lifted his own shackled arms and shouted, "Hey! What about me?"

Jyn used the distraction to kick the first soldier in the gut, knocking him against the far wall. Then she punched out the second soldier and fought past the third one. If those fools were going to give her a means to escape, she planned to use it—but she didn't want to wind up stuck with them.

Jyn charged for the transport's open door, but a large Imperial security droid blocked her way. Tall and made of sturdy black metal, it stared down at her with glowing eyes. Before she could stop it, it grabbed her by the collar, then threw her hard onto the ground.

"Congratulations," it said in a synthetic male voice. "You are being rescued. Please do not resist."

Jyn decided she would listen to the droid. For now.

CHAPTER 4

AS JYN soon found out, the soldiers who'd "rescued" her were working for the Rebel Alliance. It seemed, however, that they hadn't come to free her but to imprison her someplace else. Not even a day later, they delivered her to the headquarters of the Rebel Alliance on a green moon orbiting a gas giant called Yavin. There they hauled her in front of what she guessed must have been their version of a court-martial.

A man who identified himself as General Draven oversaw the proceedings, along with another rebel leader, the gravelly voiced General Dodonna. A third man stood nearby. Dark-haired and slim with a mustache and a stubbled chin, he had the hard eyes of a man who stood ready to do whatever it took for the Alliance to win.

Draven rattled off the list of offenses the Imperials had arrested Jyn for, which impressed her not at all. She knew the crimes she'd committed.

When that was done, though, he continued. "Imagine if the Imperial authorities had found out who you really were. Jyn Erso?"

Jyn tried not to flinch at the use of her real name. If they knew that, there was no telling what else they might have on her.

"That's your given name, is it not? Jyn Erso? Daughter of Galen Erso? A known Imperial collaborator in weapons development."

That shocked her. She'd spent most of her life trying to run away from her father's reputation, and she feared what the Alliance might want from her now that they'd learned her secret.

"What is this?" she asked.

Mon Mothma—a human woman with short red hair, the one-time senator from Chandrila—stepped from the shadows to answer. "It's a chance for you to make a fresh start. We think you might be able to help us."

She turned toward the mysterious man. "This is Captain Cassian Andor, Rebel Intelligence."

Cassian stepped forward and sized Jyn up with flinty eyes. "When was the last time you were in contact with your father?"

The question surprised Jyn, and she had lost track after a lifetime on the run. "Fifteen years ago," she estimated.

"Any idea where he's been all that time?"

Jyn didn't care for where this was heading. "I like to think he's dead. Makes things easier."

"Easier than what? That he's a tool of the Imperial war machine?"

She refused to let the man rattle her. "I've never had the luxury of political opinions."

Cassian grunted at that. "Really? When was your last contact with Saw Gerrera?"

Jyn stiffened as she wondered how large their file on her was. "It's been a long time."

"He might remember you, though, wouldn't he? He might agree to meet you if you came as a friend."

Jyn decided that she was better off keeping her mouth shut. No sense in giving them more reasons to hang her.

General Draven stepped forward though and said, "We're up against the clock here, girl. So if there's nothing to talk about, we'll just put you back where we found you. . . ."

That prodded Jyn's lips open. "I was a child. Saw Gerrera saved my life. He raised me. But I've no idea where he is. I haven't seen him in years."

"We know where to find him," said Cassian. "That's not our problem. What we need is someone who gets us through the door without being killed."

Jyn gave him a hard look, confused. "You're all rebels, aren't you?"

"Saw Gerrera's been fighting his own war for quite some time," said Mon Mothma. "He's created a great many problems for the Rebellion. We have no choice now but to try and mend that broken trust."

"What does this have to do with my father?"

The ever dignified Mon Mothma gave Cassian a go-ahead nod.

"There's an Imperial defector on Jedha, a pilot. He's been held by Saw Gerrera. He's claiming the Emperor is creating a weapon with the power to destroy planets."

Cassian hesitated for a moment before driving home his final point. "The pilot says he was sent by your father."

Try as she might, Jyn could not conjure up any response to that. She didn't even hear what the rest of them said. The next thing she knew, Mon Mothma was addressing her directly.

"It would appear your father is critical to the development of this superweapon. Given the gravity of the situation and your history with Saw, we're hoping that he'll help us locate your father and return him to the Senate for testimony."

As she spoke, Mon Mothma glanced at another person Jyn

recognized from the news: Bail Organa, the senator from Alderaan. Jyn had heard rumors that Organa was secretly working with the Alliance, and she supposed his presence confirmed it.

"And if I do it?" Jyn asked.

"We'll make sure you go free."

Jyn didn't have any loyalty to the Empire or the Alliance, but she liked the idea of being able to leave them both behind. If helping the rebels find Saw and perhaps her father was what it took, then that was what she would do.

CHAPTER 5

CASSIAN ESCORTED Jyn back to her rescuers' U-wing gunship, which sat ready to fly on the tarmac outside of the hangar. He wasn't particularly thrilled about being forced to take her along on this mission, but he didn't see how he could accomplish it without her. Saw Gerrera and his forces would otherwise shoot him on sight.

It wasn't just that she wasn't a rebel soldier or a spy. He'd dealt with many such amateurs before. But she didn't care a bit about the Rebellion, and that, he worried, might come back to bite them all.

General Draven followed them out of the hangar and called Cassian back. Cassian left Jyn in the custody of K-2SO. The reprogrammed Imperial security droid had helped free her from her prison. He could keep an eye on her for now.

The older man spoke to Cassian in a low tone, far enough away from Jyn to make sure she couldn't hear. "Galen Erso is vital to the Empire's weapons program. There will be no 'extraction.' You find him, you kill him. Then and there."

Cassian made sure to keep his expression neutral. He didn't want General Draven to know about his distaste for such orders. Cassian would kill if necessary, but he didn't like being ordered to assassinate someone.

And he didn't want Jyn to see that on his face, either.

When Cassian joined Jyn and K-2SO in the U-wing, Jyn was already glaring at the droid, who had sat down at the starship's controls.

"You met Kay-Tu?"

"Charming."

"He tends to say whatever comes into his circuits. It's a by-product of the reprogram."

"Why does she get a blaster and I don't?" K-2SO called back from the cockpit.

"What?" Cassian shot Jyn a cold look. Who would have given her a weapon? A better question: from where had she stolen it?

"I know how to use it," she told him with a smug look.

"That's what I'm afraid of." The last thing he needed was for her to shoot him in the back and escape. He held out his hand. "Give it to me."

She sat back and refused. "We're going to Jedha. That's a war zone. Trust goes both ways."

She had a point, and she was determined to be stubborn about it. He didn't have the time or the energy to argue with her. He knew she already had a pair of truncheons tucked inside her jacket, anyway. What more was a blaster?

He gave her a shrug and sat down next to K-2SO in the cockpit.

The droid couldn't believe it.

"You're letting her keep it?"

Cassian didn't want to discuss it. He started the preflight check.

"Are you interested in the probability of her using it against you?"

Cassian said nothing, hoping the literal-minded droid would take a hint for once.

"It's high."

Cassian did his best to ignore K-2SO. "Let's get going."

"It's very high."

CHAPTER 6

BODHI ROOK was having an awful day. He'd finally managed to pull off a plan weeks in the making to escape and betray the Empire, but he'd spent so long as an Imperial pilot that the people Galen Erso had sent him to didn't believe a word he told them.

The supposed rebels he'd found had turned him over to a hairless Tognath mercenary they called Two Tubes. Bodhi figured he'd gotten the name because of the breathing apparatus he needed to survive in what Bodhi thought of as perfectly acceptable air. Two Tubes could allegedly take Bodhi to Saw Gerrera, the man Galen had given Bodhi a message for. Instead of greeting Bodhi as a friend, though, Two Tubes had insisted on tying him up and pulling a sack over his head. Then the supposed rebels had marched him away to someplace far off, abusing him the entire way.

Now they had him kneeling on a rough stone floor while a man raged nearby. It was all he could do not to tremble.

"Lies!" the angry man said. "Deceptions!"

The others in the room snapped to their feet, and Bodhi wondered if this was it. Would they shoot him as a traitor before he even had a chance to deliver his message?

"Let's see it."

After a moment's pause, the man spoke again. "Bodhi Rook. Cargo pilot."

His captors hauled him to his feet. He sensed the man right in front of him. He could smell his sickly breath.

"Local boy, huh?"

Two Tubes responded in Tognath, but Bodhi understood him just fine. "There was this. It was found in his boot when he was captured."

That must have been the holochip Galen had given Bodhi!

"Okay! I can hear you! He didn't capture me." Bodhi nodded in the direction of Two Tubes's voice. "I came here myself! I defected!"

The man in front of him wasn't impressed. "Every day, more lies."

Bodhi knew his life depended on convincing that man to take him to Saw Gerrera. Saw would see through all this. He'd watch Galen's message, and he'd know Bodhi was one of the good guys. Right?

"Lies? Why would I risk everything for a lie? We don't have the time for this! I have to speak to Saw Gerrera before it's too—"

Right then, someone pulled the sack off Bodhi's head, and he realized that the man in front of him—the one he was already shouting at—could only be Saw Gerrera. His face was old and worn. He had white in his beard, and an oxygen mask hung from the front of his armor.

"Okay. You're, um . . ." Bodhi brought his voice down and nodded at the holochip in Saw's hand. "That's for you."

He glared at Two Tubes. "And I gave it to them," he added. "They did not find it! I gave it to them."

Saw didn't say a thing. He just fixed Bodhi with a dead-eyed stare.

"Galen Erso." Bodhi hoped those were the magic words that would persuade Saw they were both on the same side. "He told me to find you."

23

Saw put his oxygen mask on his face and took a deep breath from it, never taking his eyes off Bodhi. As he exhaled, Bodhi could see how much it hurt him. It was clear that something had nearly destroyed Saw, but he seemed to be clinging to his defiance—of the Empire, of death—as hard as he could.

Saw said two words to Two Tubes. A name, Bodhi thought, although one he'd never heard before.

"Bor Gullet."

"'Bor Gullet'?" The sack came down over Bodhi's head again, and someone started to drag him away. "What? Wait! No, no, wait! Galen Erso sent me!"

But Saw and his friends didn't care one bit.

CHAPTER 7

DIRECTOR ORSON KRENNIC strode through the halls of the Imperial Star Destroyer *Executrix*, his cape flowing behind him, his elite squadron of death troopers hot on his heels. This should have been a moment of triumph for him, but instead he had to deal with traitors and bureaucrats, people who meant to trip him up at every chance and take him down.

The rebels were one challenge. But that day he had to handle someone who meant to do something even worse to him: steal the glory for his accomplishments.

Wilhuff Tarkin—the Imperial governor of the Outer Rim and now a grand moff—had summoned Krennic to the bridge of his Star Destroyer. Despite the fact that the firing array was being fitted into the Death Star at that very moment, Krennic had been compelled to obey.

Once Krennic arrived on the bridge, Tarkin set into him without ceremony. This was meant to signal how much trouble Krennic was already in.

"Most unfortunate about the security breach on Jedha, Director Krennic. After so many setbacks and delays—and now this."

Krennic opened his mouth to protest, but Tarkin wouldn't let him get in a word.

"Apparently you've lost a rather talkative cargo pilot. If the Senate gets wind of our project, countless systems will flock to the Rebellion."

Krennic suppressed the urge to snarl at the Grand Moff.

The man had the Emperor's ear, and a word from him could be a huge blow to Krennic's career.

"When the battle station is finished, Grand Moff Tarkin, the Senate will be of little concern."

After all, who would stand up to a weapon able to destroy an entire planet in a matter of moments? The Senate would fall apart almost instantly. That was the whole point of building the Death Star in the first place.

If Krennic's words impressed Tarkin, the man refused to show it. "*When* has become *now*, Director Krennic. The Emperor will tolerate no further delay. You have made time an ally of the Rebellion."

Krennic's blood rose at the accusation and all it implied. He wanted to turn the Death Star on Tarkin's Star Destroyer and see how much of a failure the Emperor might consider him then.

Tarkin shot down that idea with a condescending smirk, almost as if he could read Krennic's mind. "I suggest we solve both problems simultaneously with an immediate test of the weapon. Failure will find you explaining *why* to a far less patient audience."

Krennic steeled himself. "I will not fail," he told the Grand Moff.

He knew he had more on the line with this test than merely his career. He was also betting his life on it. With all the problems the project had suffered so far, he could only hope he was right.

CHAPTER 8

JEDHA CITY wasn't exactly what Jyn had expected. She supposed that once, long before, it had been a beautiful city that glowed with the power of the Force, but it had fallen on hard times. It sat on a high plateau in the middle of a deep valley, surrounded by an ancient wall that had protected it from ground invasion for countless centuries.

Many of the proud spires that once stabbed into the sky, though, had been shattered, and much of the rest of the city lay under a thick layer of dust and smoke generated by years of conflict. To top it all off, almost the entire city was under the shadow of an Imperial Star Destroyer that hovered over it.

Jyn had rarely seen such a raw display of power, and she could only imagine what it must have been like for the residents to wake up one day to find themselves living under it.

"What's with the Destroyer?" she asked Cassian as they surveyed the city from a distance.

"The Empire's been sending those since Saw Gerrera started attacking their cargo shipments."

Jyn noticed several such ships running back and forth from the Star Destroyer to various points within the city.

"What are they bringing in?"

"It's what they're bringing out. Kyber crystal. All they can get. We believe the Empire is using it as fuel for the weapon."

"The weapon your father is building," K-2SO observed.

Jyn looked askance at the droid. "Maybe we should leave Target Practice behind."

The droid took half a step back, as if shocked. "Are you talking about me?"

Jyn wondered if the machine might get angry with her, but Cassian intervened. "She's right. We need to blend in. Stay with the ship."

"I can blend in," the droid protested. "I'm an Imperial droid. The city is under Imperial occupation."

Jyn could hardly believe it, but the Imperial security droid seemed offended. "Half the people here want to reprogram you. The other half want to put a hole in your head."

"I'm surprised you're so concerned with my safety."

"I'm not. I'm just worried they might miss you and hit me."

Jyn walked away, intending to end the conversation at that point, but the droid couldn't resist one last dig as she and Cassian began their hike to Jedha City.

"Doesn't sound so bad to me."

CHAPTER 9

BODHI KNEW he was going to hate this. Saw Gerrera's rebels had finally managed to scrape up that Bor Gullet they were talking about, and to prepare him for it they'd strapped him to a chair so tightly he could barely feel his arms. Then they'd sent the creature into Bodhi's rough and dirty prison cell.

Bor was like nothing Bodhi had ever seen. It resembled a sea creature, with more tentacles than Bodhi cared to count, but it moved about on dry land rather than in the water. Bodhi wasn't sure how they'd even managed to get Bor into the rebel hideout much less into his cell. The creature seemed to defy everything Bodhi knew about how living things fit into spaces.

To make everything worse, Saw Gerrera stood just outside the door to Bodhi's cell, explaining everything that was about to happen to him.

"Bor Gullet can feel your thoughts. No lie is safe."

Bodhi wanted to protest, to swear to Saw that none of this was necessary, that he'd already told him the truth. But he knew it would do no good. He'd already tried to convince Saw and his rebels of that fact so many times, and they'd absolutely refused to believe anything he told them. He'd screamed himself hoarse.

There was nothing for him to do but submit to this creature and its powers. The thought of having such a thing rummage through his mind appalled him, but he didn't see what else he could do. If he could have turned back time, he might have decided not to defect, not to help Galen Erso, not to try to save the galaxy.

But it was far too late.

The creature's tentacles reached for Bodhi. He strained against his bonds, unable to resist cringing away from it as he fought the urge to vomit.

"What have you really brought me, cargo pilot?" Saw asked in his raspy voice. "Bor Gullet will know the truth."

One of Bor's tentacles snaked out and wrapped around Bodhi's throat. He wanted to scream, but the tentacle had already started to constrict so tight he couldn't draw enough air. Pulling away from the creature only made it worse.

More tentacles reached out then, wrapping around Bodhi's head. Their suckers attached to precise points on Bodhi's temples, and he could feel them pulsing, almost as if they were milking his brain.

Saw's voice was the last thing Bodhi heard before his mind began to scramble into static and white noise. The man said something Bodhi could only hope wouldn't come true.

"The unfortunate side effect of Bor Gullet's techniques is that one tends to lose one's mind."

CHAPTER 10

JEDHA CITY didn't impress Jyn up close any more than it had from a distance. The city bore all the clear signs of a longstanding Imperial occupation: shattered shells of buildings scattered about the landscape, blaster-fire scorch marks marring the still-intact walls, and anti-Palpatine graffiti decorating most other surfaces.

As she followed Cassian through the city's ancient streets, gazing at the wear and tear of impending war all around her, she brushed up against a grizzled man with a disfigured face.

"Hey! You better watch yourself!"

Jyn put her hand on her blaster as the man and his Aqualish pal turned to confront her. If the two were spoiling for a brawl, she wasn't averse to obliging them.

Cassian intervened, though, and pulled her away. The two men glared after her. Maybe it was the Imperial hologram nearby, shouting out demands of loyalty to the Empire, that convinced the men Jedha wasn't the right place to pick a fight.

More specifically, the hologram called for the citizens of Jedha to come forward with any information about a missing cargo pilot. That had to be the same man Jyn and Cassian had gone to find, which would only make their impossible job that much harder.

Cassian didn't seem to let that deter him though. He moved like a man with a purpose.

"I had a contact, one of Saw's rebels, but he's just gone missing," he said. "His sister will be looking for him. The Temple's been destroyed, but she'll be there waiting. We'll give her your name and hope that gets us a meeting."

"Hope?" Jyn didn't like to depend on something so ridiculous.

"Rebellions are built on hope," Cassian said.

As they weaved through the crowded streets, Cassian spotted someone he recognized. "Wait for me," he ordered Jyn as he strode ahead.

While Cassian spoke to a bearded man in a food stall, Jyn tried to listen in but couldn't manage it over the noise of people thronging the streets. Instead, she realized that she was hearing a different voice.

She glanced around and spotted the owner of that voice: a man dressed in monk's robes. His eyes were a pale blue, and he seemed to be addressing no one in particular—perhaps everyone—as he repeated over and over, "May the Force of others be with you. . . . May the Force of others be with you. . . ." Jyn realized he was blind.

The man's droning fell silent for a moment, and then he said, "Would you trade that necklace for a glimpse of your future?"

Jyn froze. The blind man wasn't looking at her, but then he wasn't looking at anyone, was he? She was wearing a necklace, the kyber crystal her mother had given her so long before, but it was hidden under her shirt. There was no way he could know about it.

"Yes," he said, seeming to sense her confusion. "I'm talking to you."

She fixed him with a hard look she soon realized he couldn't see.

"I am Chirrut Îmwe."

"How did you know I was wearing a necklace?"

The man almost smiled. "For that answer, you must pay."

Jyn noticed another man standing behind the monk. He seemed to be the opposite of Chirrut. He wore a red chest plate of armor rather than robes, and his hair was long and shaggy. Somehow, though, the two seemed perfectly matched, like brothers who'd each gone a different way.

"What do you know of kyber crystals?" Chirrut asked.

Jyn wasn't sure how to respond. Was this some kind of scam? "My father. He said they powered the Jedi lightsabers."

Cassian must have finished his conversation, because he chose that moment to pull Jyn away from the monk.

Chirrut called after her as she left. "The strongest stars have hearts of kyber."

"We're not here to make friends," Cassian told her as he dragged her away. "Not with those guys."

Mystified and intrigued, Jyn glanced back at the two men as she and Cassian departed. "Who are they?"

"The Guardians of the Whills. Protectors of the Kyber Temple. But there's nothing left to protect, so now they're just causing trouble for everybody."

Something had changed with Cassian. "You seem awfully tense all of a sudden."

"We have to hurry," he said. "This town—it's ready to blow."

CHAPTER 11

JYN FOLLOWED Cassian through the streets of Jedha until they reached the Holy Quarter in the heart of the ancient city, and her disaster radar instantly went off. She glanced about and saw a number of things coming together at once.

A cargo shuttle dropped out of the sky, racing from the Star Destroyer hovering above and blocking out the sun. At about the same time, a treaded Imperial assault tank turned onto the street, coming to protect the shuttle.

People started scurrying about, which was a perfectly natural reaction to such a display of Imperial force. To Jyn's eye, though, some of the people weren't fleeing. They were gathering closer.

"Tell me you have a backup plan," she said to Cassian.

"We've got to get out of here."

It wasn't much of a plan, but Jyn was all for it. She didn't want to be anywhere nearby when whatever was about to happen happened.

But it was already too late.

One of the people who'd been attracted by the tank's arrival plucked a grenade from somewhere and hurled it at the tank. It went off with a bang that set Jyn's ears ringing. The blast destroyed the tank's treads, and it came to a grinding halt.

Many of the others who'd been creeping closer produced blasters and opened fire on the stormtroopers escorting the tank down the street. Most of them were human, but one was a Tognath soldier with tubes snaking out of the breathing mask he wore over his mouth.

The stormtroopers returned fire, and the street transformed into a shooting gallery.

Jyn and Cassian pressed themselves into a doorway. Jyn drew her blaster, happy that Cassian hadn't tried to confiscate it from her before. "Looks like we found Saw's rebels," she said.

She didn't recognize any of them, of course. It had been years since she'd seen Saw, and soldiers tended not to survive in his outfit for long. They had, after all, committed to the most dangerous cause in the galaxy: struggling to free it from the Emperor's grasp.

The tank might not have been able to move, but that didn't mean it was defenseless. Its side cannons swiveled, hunting for a target as rebels on a nearby roof fired down on it.

Jyn spotted a young girl huddled in front of the building, and she realized that the tank was about to fire at it in an effort to blast the rebels off the roof. Without thinking, Jyn darted forward, ignoring Cassian, who called after her. She hunkered down over the girl and shielded her from the blast as the tank's first round went off.

The shot smashed into the building, blasting away the front of it. As the debris tumbled down around her, Jyn scooped the girl up and found the child's mother already racing over to take her away. Jyn handed off the girl to her grateful parent and then dove after them, trying to avoid the tank's next shot.

Cassian, to his credit, opened fire to give Jyn cover. She just wasn't sure at first what he was shooting at, as his shots seemed high. She glanced up to see a rebel toppling off the building, a fresh grenade in his hand. As he landed among his fellow rebels, the grenade exploded, killing not only him but several others.

Cold as it might be, Jyn could only think, *Better them than me.* She ran up to Cassian and was about to thank him when she saw another grenade rolling toward the tank. She dove forward, taking Cassian to the ground with her. They avoided the brunt of the blast, which transformed the tank into a smoldering hulk.

Cassian leaped to his feet and raced away, and Jyn followed straight after him. He led them into an alley and then came to a skidding halt when he saw an entire squad of stormtroopers blocking their way.

He spun on his heel and ran back the other way, passing Jyn. "This way!"

Jyn had already had enough of running from the Empire. After facing down one of their tanks, she wasn't about to let those clowns in their fancy armor run her off. She pulled a pair of truncheons from her jacket and set to work.

With the stormtroopers' attention on Cassian, she was able to take down the first two of them before they knew she was a threat. The next two required a bit more effort, but they proved no match for her. She attacked them the way she preferred: fast and strong, before they could hit her back.

The last two, though, were smart enough to back up a bit and ready their rifles. While they were still waiting for their compatriots to get clear of her—or fall at her feet, as they soon did—she drew her blaster and began firing.

As Jyn took down the remainder of the stormtrooper squad, she heard something stomping up behind her. She spun about and spotted an Imperial security droid looming over her, and she took it down with a single shot to the chest.

The droid toppled over, smoking from its wound and revealing another security droid behind it. "Did you know that wasn't me?" it said.

Realizing that the second droid was K-2SO, Jyn lowered her weapon. After a perhaps too long moment, she answered, "Of course."

Cassian returned then to chew the droid out. "I thought I told you to stay on the ship." He stared at the stormtroopers scattered about the alley. None of them stirred.

"You did. But I thought it was boring and you were in trouble. There are a lot of explosions for two people blending in."

Cassian seemed ready to lay into the droid again, despite the thing's logic, but K-2SO cut him off. "The Imperial forces are converging on our present location."

Jyn didn't see one of the downed stormtroopers reach for a grenade on his belt and activate it, and neither did Cassian. Fortunately, though, when the trooper threw it at her, K-2SO plucked it out of the air as if he and the trooper had been playing catch. The droid then tossed it back at the stormtrooper, and the grenade put an end to any worries about him or his squad mates getting back up again.

"I suggest we leave immediately," K-2SO said. Jyn couldn't think of a single reason to argue with him.

CHAPTER 12

JYN, CASSIAN, and K-2SO moved through the streets of the Holy Quarter. They tried not to break into a run, for fear of drawing attention to themselves. For a moment, Jyn thought they might make it out of the city without any more troubles.

Then they found their way blocked by an X-wing starfighter that had somehow crashed into the street. It looked like it had been abandoned there as a lost cause, too much trouble to try to move.

Jyn had seen stormtroopers marching rebel pilots through the streets earlier in the day. She wondered if one of them had managed to eject from this wreck.

As Jyn glanced about for a better way out, another patrol of stormtroopers—a dozen of them this time—approached.

"Halt!" the commander said. "Stop right there."

They all froze, unsure of what to do. Jyn started looking for which stormtroopers she should shoot first. Or would she be better off running instead? She considered using K-2SO as a shield, but the droid was so tall and his legs were so long that he was almost useless in that regard.

"Where are you taking these prisoners?" the commander asked.

"These are prisoners." K-2SO barely managed to make that sound like it wasn't a question.

"Yes, where are you taking them?"

Jyn wanted to answer for the droid, but she feared that

would make it look like she *wasn't* a prisoner, and at the moment that was working to their advantage.

"I am taking them . . ." K-2SO started to figure that same thing out. "To imprison them. In prison."

Cassian ran out of patience at that moment and tried to cut in. "He's taking us to—"

Much to Jyn's surprise, K-2SO smacked Cassian across the mouth. "Quiet! And there's a fresh one if you mouth off again."

It seemed the droid could sell a deception once he understood what he was supposed to be lying about.

"We'll take them from here," the commander said. The stormtroopers moved in to make that happen.

K-2SO did his best to talk the commander out of it. "That's okay. If you could just point me in the right direction, I can take them, I'm sure. I've taken them this far."

Despite the droid's protests, the stormtroopers placed shackles on Jyn and Cassian.

"Hey, hey, droid. Wait a second." Cassian tried to get K-2SO to stand up to the stormtroopers, but the commander wasn't having any of it.

"Take them away."

"You can't take them away," K-2SO said.

The commander looked the droid up and down. "You stay here. We need to check your diagnostics."

K-2SO was indignant. "Diagnostics? I'm capable of running my own diagnostics, thank you very much."

Off to the side, someone called out, "Let them pass in peace!"

Jyn—along with everyone else in the street—turned to see the odd blind monk she'd met before, sitting in a doorway. *His* name *was* Chirrut, *right?* He unfolded himself and got to his feet, his walking stick in one hand. He approached the troopers as if he knew exactly where they were.

"Let them pass in peace," he said again, as if to confirm that he was the one who'd called out in the first place. Then he began chanting a prayer Jyn had never heard before.

"The Force is with me. And I am in the Force. And I fear nothing. For all is as the Force wills it."

The commander didn't care for that at all. "Hey, stop right there!"

One of the stormtroopers leaned over to explain the monk's behavior to the commander. "He's blind."

"Is he deaf?" The commander raised his rifle and aimed it right at the monk. "I said, stop right there!"

CHAPTER 13

CHIRRUT JUKED to the left as he approached, and the commander's blaster bolt zipped right past him. Cassian dove for cover, and Jyn followed suit. If this mad monk was going to sacrifice his life for them, she planned to take advantage of it.

She didn't have to worry about Chirrut though. The monk swept in close to the stormtroopers—too close for them to fire at him again—and began swinging his walking stick. He smacked down one trooper with a blow to the head and then came around and swept another off his feet.

One of the stormtroopers fired a desperate shot at Chirrut, but the monk dodged it again. The bolt struck a stormtrooper behind him instead, almost as if he'd planned it that way.

The monk kept up this blur of action until every one of the stormtroopers lay at his feet. Jyn could only watch in astonishment as he worked. She almost felt like she should applaud when he was done.

Unfortunately, another squad of stormtroopers rushed in at that point. This group was too far away for Chirrut to attack with his stick, and they could already see how dangerous he was. They weren't going to give him a chance to get close enough to hurt them.

Before the new arrivals could open fire, though, a raggedy soldier stepped out from the other side of the street and blew them away. Jyn recognized him as the man who'd been standing behind Chirrut before. If he'd looked dangerous then, he proved it now, taking down each of the stormtroopers with a barrage of well-placed shots.

When he was done, the soldier strolled across the street and handed the blind monk a lightbow. Jyn wondered how Chirrut could hope to use it, but he held it like he'd been born to it.

"You almost shot me," Chirrut said to the soldier.

The soldier grunted at him. "You're welcome."

A stormtrooper who wasn't smart enough to play dead began to stir, and the soldier shot him again. He gave the stormtrooper a firm *stay down* nod, then glanced around to scan for other threats.

"Clear of hostiles," K-2SO reported as Jyn and Cassian got to their feet.

The soldier aimed his blaster at the droid.

K-2SO corrected himself. "One hostile!"

Jyn moved forward to keep the soldier from shooting the droid. "He's with us!"

The soldier hesitated. He glanced at Chirrut for confirmation, and the monk told him, "No. They're okay."

The soldier reluctantly shouldered his weapon. K-2SO proceeded to ignore the man while he let Jyn and Cassian loose from their shackles.

Jyn thanked the droid. She still couldn't put all her trust in K-2SO, but he clearly cared about Cassian and—by extension—her.

Cassian, however, wasn't quite as impressed. "Go back to the ship," he said to the droid, not bothering to hide his annoyance at the way K-2SO had disobeyed his previous order. "Wait for my call."

The droid did as he was instructed. Cassian nodded toward Chirrut and asked the soldier, "Is he Jedi?"

The thought had occurred to Jyn, too. The way the blind man moved seemed impossible—at least for someone who couldn't manipulate the Force.

The soldier gave Cassian a firm shake of his head. "No Jedi anymore. Only dreamers like this fool."

Chirrut protested his friend's opinion. "The Force *did* protect me."

The soldier pointed at himself. "*I* protected you."

They didn't have time for this. They'd already run into more stormtroopers than Jyn cared to count, and if they stuck around, more were sure to find them. "Can you get us to Saw Gerrera?" she asked.

As if in answer, a group of rebels emerged, their weapons leveled at Jyn, Cassian, K-2SO, and their rescuers. "Hands in the air!" one of them said.

Under other circumstances, Jyn might have tried to escape. After all, Chirrut and his friend had made quick work of the stormtroopers, and she and Cassian could handle themselves pretty well. The rebels probably worked with Saw though.

Chirrut didn't want to give in to the rebels. "Can't you see we are no friends of the Empire?" He motioned to the downed stormtroopers scattered about the place, as if that should be plenty of evidence.

The Tognath whom Jyn had seen lurking about earlier stepped up then and shouted at them in his native tongue. "Tell that to the one who killed our men!"

Jyn understood him, and she mentally cursed. The tube-faced man must have been referring to when Cassian had shot

43

a grenade-toting rebel to save her life. She'd wondered if that would come back to haunt them.

She stepped forward and shouted as clearly as she could, "Anyone who kills me or my friends will answer to Saw Gerrera!"

"And why is that?" the Tognath said.

Jyn hesitated only the slightest bit. It had been a long time since she'd said the words out loud. "Because I am the daughter of Galen Erso."

The Tognath *didn't* hesitate. "Take them!"

The rebels stormed toward Jyn and the others, stripping them of their weapons and throwing bags over their heads so they couldn't see.

"Are you kidding me?" Chirrut said, exasperated. "I'm blind!"

CHAPTER 14

CASSIAN MIGHT have been in worse spots than this one. He just couldn't remember when. He only hoped that when they finally reached the rebels' hideout, Jyn wouldn't sell him out to Saw Gerrera.

It would be so easy for her to deny him and his mission and just have Saw kill him. That would be tragic in many ways, and not just for him personally.

But he'd already made the decision to trust her, whether that proved to be a wise choice or not. That's why he'd let her keep her blaster. And why he hadn't said a thing to her about the truncheons she carried.

He knew that his life would be in her hands sooner or later. If he was going to have to trust her in a situation like this, it seemed petty to complain about her carrying weapons.

That didn't mean he wasn't worried though. From the reports he'd read about Jyn, she was a hardened criminal with a long list of transgressions—and not only against the Empire. He was depending on her better nature.

That and the fact that he was helping her find her long-lost father.

He hoped at least one of those things would work in his favor.

Saw's rebels didn't care about any of that, of course. That was at least partly Cassian's fault, he had to admit. He hadn't wanted to kill any of them, but he hadn't seen any other choice. Not if he wanted to protect Jyn like he needed to.

The rebels took the sack off Cassian's head once they finally got inside their hideout. It was a rough place that looked like it had been carved out of one of Jedha's many systems of caves, and the people who filled it looked just as hard and mean.

A large rebel threw Cassian into a cell alongside the blind monk and his efficiently violent friend. As Cassian got a better look at the place, he realized the rebels had set up their base inside an ossuary, an ancient burial place for the monks of Jedha. Their bones lined every bit of the walls, even in the cell.

Once their captors retreated, Cassian picked himself up and leaned against the cell door to scope out as much as he could see. He spotted a couple of rebels arguing over a game of dejarik. They played with carved wooden pieces on an old table rather than on the regular holotable.

The monk settled down and began chanting. Cassian hoped he would eventually give up, but he seemed tireless.

After a while, Chirrut's soldier friend finally took notice of the chanting. He looked over at the monk in disbelief and said, "You pray?"

Chirrut didn't break the rhythm of his chanting for even an instant.

The soldier shook his head at him. "You pray."

He allowed himself a bitter chuckle and then turned to Cassian. "He's praying for the door to open."

That got the monk's attention. "It bothers him because he knows it is possible."

The soldier laughed out loud at that.

Chirrut nodded toward his friend, but he spoke to Cassian. "Baze Malbus was once the most devoted Guardian of us all."

That surprised Cassian. The soldier had once been a monk like Chirrut? Had it been the Imperial occupation of Jedha that had so changed him? If so, how had Chirrut maintained his faith while Baze had so completely abandoned it?

Cassian didn't care to take sides in their ongoing argument. Still, he couldn't help commenting. "I'm beginning to think the Force and I have different priorities."

"Relax, Captain," Chirrut said. "We've been in worse cages than this one."

Cassian glanced around at the walls and the cell door. "Yeah? Well, this is a first for me."

"There is more than one sort of prison, Captain. I sense that you carry yours wherever you go."

Cassian looked away. The remark jabbed him harder than he cared to let on.

CHAPTER 15

SAW'S REBELS escorted Jyn into a long, cavernous room, still part of the ancient burial ground for the monks of Jedha. Light streamed in through a large window carved into the wall, and she could see the wide valley spreading beyond it, with Jedha City rising in the distance and basking in the sun.

It took Jyn a moment to realize something was different about that picture. The Imperial Star Destroyer that had been looming over the city was gone.

She didn't know what that meant, and she didn't have time to ponder it. She spied Saw Gerrera across the room, and thoughts of all else fled.

"Is it really you?" Saw said. His voice was weaker, raspier than she remembered. "I can't believe it."

He went toward her, walking with a new limp. His once bald head was covered in gray hair. He wore an oxygen mask around his neck.

"Must be quite a surprise," she said, unable to contain her frustration with him.

The sharp tone of her voice stopped him short. He gave her a tentative look. "Are we not friends?"

Jyn wasn't sure what he could possibly mean by that. "The last time I saw you, you gave me a knife and loaded blaster and told me to wait in a bunker until daylight."

"I knew you were safe."

That's not the point, she thought. "You left me behind."

He frowned. "You were already the best soldier in my cadre."

Thin compliments were not going to get him off the hook. "I was sixteen!"

"I was protecting you."

By leaving me behind? She thought she'd gotten over how much that had hurt her years before, but the sight of the man— the way he dismissed her concerns—brought it all flooding back. "You dumped me."

"You were the daughter of an Imperial science officer. People were starting to figure that out. People who wanted to use you as a hostage."

Jyn glared at him. She'd known all that, of course. She just hadn't thought he'd ever give in to it.

"Not a day goes by I don't think of you." He gave her a rueful look. "But *today* of all days . . ."

Saw sized her up, and Jyn wondered if he would find her wanting.

"It's a trap, isn't it?" he said.

"What?" The question confused Jyn at first. Then she realized it wasn't about her at all. It was about him. Him and his paranoia.

"The pilot. The message. All of it."

Saw reached down for his oxygen mask and took a long pull on it. It saddened Jyn to see him in such a state. He'd always been so strong, almost like a force of nature.

He narrowed his eyes, gazing at her like a cornered beast. "Did they send you . . . ? Have you come here to kill me?" He allowed himself a half-hearted chuckle and gestured to himself. "There's not much left."

Jyn gave him a pitiful shake of her head. "I don't care enough to kill you, Saw."

As the words left her lips, she knew them to be true. She'd spent years proving herself independent enough not to need the man's help. She hadn't forgiven him, but she'd done her best to forget him. Until now.

"So what is it, Jyn?" Saw asked, both suspicious and confused.

Jyn didn't see any reason to lie. Saw would see right through her if she tried.

"The Alliance wants my father. They think he's sent you a message about a weapon. I guess they think by sending me you might actually help them out."

Saw nodded, clearly weighing her words against a lifetime of paranoid habits that had kept him alive till then. She wondered if he would believe her, but she realized she didn't care. She'd done what she could. The rest was up to him.

"So what is it that you want, Jyn?"

"To be left alone." She permitted herself a bitter smile. That was true, although she wasn't sure if it was possible. Maybe not anymore. But she had to try.

"They wanted an introduction," she said. "They've got it. I'm out now. The rest of you can do what you want."

"You care not about the cause?"

The idea that he would bring up his *glorious* cause at a moment like that appalled Jyn. "The cause? *Seriously?*" She gawked at him. "The Alliance? The rebels? Whatever it is you're calling yourself these days? All it's ever brought me is pain."

That set Saw back on his heels. Jyn knew he thought he'd indoctrinated her as a good little rebel during their years together. The way he'd abandoned her, though, had crushed that part of her soul.

"You can stand to see the Imperial flag reign across the galaxy?"

"It's not a problem if you don't look up," she told him.

Saw stiffened at that. Her words had cut him deep. She might have felt bad about that if he hadn't already hurt her far worse.

He blinked at her for a moment, then nodded. "I have something to show you."

CHAPTER 16

THE SHADOW of the Death Star fell over Jedha, and Krennic reveled in the sight. He'd worked so hard to get that far—to make the battle station operational—and his moment of triumph was finally within his grasp. The presence of Grand Moff Tarkin, though, prevented him from fully enjoying it.

"The Emperor is awaiting my report on what transpires here," Tarkin said, as if they didn't both know that and what he really meant.

Tarkin considered the Death Star to be his project, despite the fact that it would never have happened without Krennic. He was like the man who bought a landspeeder and paraded around in it as if he'd created it.

If Krennic could have gotten away with it, he'd have tossed Tarkin out of one of the Death Star's airlocks. Instead, he did as he always had and showed Tarkin a respect he didn't feel. "One had hoped that he and Lord Vader might have been here for such an occasion."

Tarkin almost clucked his tongue at Krennic. "I thought it prudent to save you from any potential embarrassment."

Krennic knew that meant Tarkin wanted to oversee the Death Star's initial operations by himself, to make sure it was in working order before he attempted to take over. Otherwise, he couldn't be sure that he didn't need Krennic any longer. But Krennic was far too wise to let the man get rid of him that easily.

"Your concern is hardly warranted," he told Tarkin.

Tarkin smirked at him. "If saying it would only make it so."

Krennic wondered exactly how much the Emperor would miss his favorite grand moff should he suddenly disappear. He decided to ignore the dig and address the rest of the people in the room instead.

"All Imperial forces have been evacuated, and I stand ready to destroy the entire moon."

Tarkin arched an eyebrow at Krennic. "That won't be necessary. We need a statement, not a manifesto. The Holy City will be enough for today."

Krennic stifled a retort. He knew now what the Grand Moff's game was. He would take over the Death Star once Krennic had proved it would work. And then he would take credit for using it to annihilate an entire planet.

Krennic promised himself he would find a way to leave Tarkin disappointed in that regard. For the moment, though, he still needed to play along with the Grand Moff's power grab.

He moved to the Death Star's command console and issued his order. "Target Jedha City," he said. "Prepare single reactor ignition."

That would be enough to wipe the ancient city from the face of the moon. If only the Emperor—or even his emissary, Lord Vader—had been there to bear witness to the destruction. As it was, news of Krennic's triumph would only reach them through Tarkin, who would be sure to take as much of the credit as he could.

Krennic strove not to let such personal setbacks color the moment. Either way, he had a job to do.

"Fire when ready."

CHAPTER 17

CASSIAN COULD sense they were running out of time. Jyn had been gone far too long. If she was going to convince Saw Gerrera to free them, shouldn't someone have come down to release them by now?

He kept watch on the guards, looking for any sign from them as to how things with Jyn and Saw were going. If all went poorly, he would have to lead a desperate attempt to escape. Otherwise, they would all be executed for sure.

"Who's the one in the next cell?" Chirrut asked out of nowhere.

Cassian hadn't given any thought to their neighbor. He'd been too preoccupied with the guards.

"What?" Baze said. "Where?"

Baze walked toward the bars separating them from a man huddled in the darkness. Baze peered at him and then curled up his lips as if tasting something foul. "An Imperial pilot."

That caught Cassian's attention. After all, they'd gone to Jedha in search of an Imperial pilot. Had Saw really thrown the defector into a cell, too?

"Pilot?"

Baze moved closer to the adjoining cell. "I'll kill him."

"No!" Cassian dashed over to pull Baze back. "Wait! No!"

Baze wasn't the sort to just let someone push him aside, but Cassian insisted. "Back off," he told the man. "Back off!"

He peered into the next cell and saw just what had gotten Baze's temper to flare up: a skinny man with olive skin, dark hair, and a thin beard. He wore the uniform of an Imperial pilot.

The man trembled as he noticed Cassian, perhaps because of Baze's threats. Or maybe something else was wrong with him on top of that.

"Okay," Cassian said softly, trying to get the pilot to calm down. "Okay."

The man's eyes rolled, and Cassian couldn't tell if his mind was still in the room with them or not. Had Saw been torturing him?

"Are you the pilot?" Cassian asked. "Hey, hey . . . Are you the pilot? The shuttle pilot?"

The man fixed him with an empty gaze. "Pilot?" The word seemed to make some sense to him, almost like it was stirring a long-buried memory.

"What's wrong with him?" Chirrut asked.

Cassian wished he knew. He'd seen people in a condition like this before, and he shuddered to think what the man had gone through to get to that point. He wasn't about to explain to Chirrut what might have happened and how it could be treated though. He needed to make sure he had the right man first.

"Galen Erso," he said to the man in the cell. "You know the name?"

The pilot sat up, but his eyes still seemed glassy. The way he moved, though—the way he blinked at Cassian now that he'd said Galen's name—that had to mean something, right?

"I brought the message," the man said. "I'm the pilot."

Cassian wanted to cheer. The man sat up fully now and focused on Cassian and the others in the next cell. "I'm the pilot. *I'm the pilot!*"

CHAPTER 18

SAW LED Jyn to a projector and inserted a holographic chip into it. He glanced out the window as if he was waiting for something, but he didn't let that stop him from working the projector.

"This is the message from the pilot," he said. He offered no preface. No explanation. He just let it play.

A flickering bluish image of Jyn's father burst to life atop the projector. She knew he must have recorded the message recently, but it seemed to her as if a ghost had leaped out of her past to talk with her. He looked older, more worn than she remembered, and she wondered exactly how life had treated him.

She couldn't tell if she felt like crying with rage or joy. But he couldn't see her either way, so she settled in to watch and listen instead.

"Saw, if you're watching this, then perhaps there is a chance to save the Alliance. Perhaps there's a chance to explain myself and, though I don't dare hope for too much, a chance for Jyn, if she's alive—if you can *possibly* find her—to let her know that my love for her has never faded, and how desperately I've missed her."

She felt her throat start to tighten. All those years she'd been apart from him—all those years she'd spent alone after Saw had abandoned her—threatened to well up and swallow her whole, but she shoved her emotions aside for the moment.

This was her father, after all, and she didn't want to miss a word of what he said.

"Jyn, my Stardust . . . I can't imagine what you think of me. When I was taken, I faced some bitter truths. I was told that, soon enough, Krennic would have you.

"As time went by, I knew that you were either dead or so well hidden that he would never find you. But I knew if I refused to work, if I took my own life, it would only be a matter of time before Krennic realized he no longer needed me to complete the project.

"So I did the one thing that nobody expected. I lied.

"Or I *learned* to lie. I played the part of a beaten man resigned to the sanctuary of his work. I made myself indispensable, and all the while I laid the groundwork of my revenge."

He paused a moment, preparing himself to reveal his deepest secret, the thing that would seal his betrayal of the Empire.

"We call it the Death Star. There is no better name.

"My colleagues, many of them, have fooled themselves into thinking they are creating something so terrifying and powerful it will never be used. But they're wrong. No weapon has ever been left on the shelf. And the day is coming soon when it will be unleashed.

"I've placed a flaw deep within the system. A scar so small and powerful they'll never find it."

He let the importance of that sink in before he continued.

"Jyn, if you're listening . . ." He stopped for a moment, clearly overwhelmed with the emotion of the idea that his daughter might still be alive. Jyn felt an answering pang in her heart.

"My beloved, so much of my life has been wasted. I try to

think of you only in the moments when I'm strong, because the pain of not having you with me—your mother, *our family* . . .

"The pain of that loss is so overwhelming, I risk failing even now. It's just so hard not to think of you. Think of where you are . . ."

Galen bowed his head for a moment. Once he raised it, Jyn could see the look of determination burning in his eyes.

"Saw. The reactor system. That's the key. That's the place I've laid my trap.

"It's unstable. So one blast to any part of it will destroy the entire station.

"You'll need the plans—the structural plans—to find your way, but they exist. I know there's at least one complete engineering archive in the data vault in the Citadel Tower on Scarif. Any pressurized explosion to the reactor module will set off a chain reaction that will—"

The message cut off. Jyn wanted to rail against it, to scream at her father to go on.

Then she realized that the problem wasn't with the recording but with the power to Saw's entire base. All the lights had gone out at the same time.

She looked out the window at Jedha City and saw why.

CHAPTER 19

CASSIAN COULD hear the destruction of Jedha City roaring outside the rebels' hideout, although he didn't know what it was at first. The noise drew the guards away from the cells, and Cassian took advantage of that to pick the lock on their cell door. The guards may have taken the obvious weapons from him, but they'd missed others, the kinds of things that Cassian relied on to get himself out of a tight pinch.

The moment Cassian got the door open, he burst out of the cell. Baze went right after him, calling for Chirrut to follow.

Cassian charged over to a table where the guards had stashed the things they'd taken from him and the others. He found his comlink and flicked it on.

"Kay-Tu! Kay-Tu! Where are you?" he shouted into it.

The droid's voice came through immediately. "There you are! I'm standing by as you ordered, though there is a problem on the horizon. There is no horizon."

Cassian felt his blood run cold. This was the worst-case scenario he'd dreaded from the moment he'd first been sent on this mission: to have the doomsday weapon he was trying to stop be turned against him.

"Lock on to my comm and locate our position!" he ordered K-2SO. "Bring that ship in here now!"

Cassian scooped up the rest of his gear and turned to see Baze and Chirrut standing behind him.

"Where are you going?" Chirrut asked.

"I've got to find Jyn," Cassian said. Then he remembered what they had gone to Jedha for in the first place.

"Get the pilot!" he said to Baze. "We need him!"

Baze didn't understand all the reasons for that, Cassian knew, but the man decided to trust him anyhow. "All right. I'll get the pilot."

Cassian didn't know if Baze meant to save the pilot or kill him. He understood the grudge the man held against Imperials, after all. But Cassian decided he didn't have time to do anything other than trust Baze, too. He sprinted off to find Jyn.

The walls of the monastery/hideout shook like a monster was trying to rattle them down. The place wouldn't hold together for much longer, Cassian knew.

He followed his instincts, rushing deeper into the place while it seemed everyone else was fleeing out. No one paid much attention to him, too busy trying to save their own lives to worry about who he might be and what he was doing there. He eventually found a large, long chamber lit by a bright light streaming through a wide window.

Jyn had fallen to her knees in front of a holographic projector that had gone dead. An older man stood next to her, trying to comfort her.

"Jyn!" Cassian said as he raced toward her. "Jyn . . ."

The man turned, and Cassian recognized him: Saw Gerrera. Under other circumstances, Cassian might have gone for his blaster, or maybe just turned and fled. Now, though, they had no time for such things.

Cassian approached Jyn from her other side. "We've got to go," he said. "I know where your father is." The pilot—Bodhi Rook, he'd said his name was—had filled him in.

"Go, Jyn!" Saw said to her. "You must go."

Jyn stood up but hesitated. She took Saw's arm as if she planned to haul the man along with them. He shook her off, though, and Cassian could see why.

He was slow, beaten, sick. No longer the legendary warrior— the terror of the Empire—he'd once been. He wasn't able to run any longer, but he wanted to make sure Jyn did.

"Save yourself. Please!"

"Come on," Cassian said as he took her by the hand. She resisted him, not willing to abandon the old man who Cassian knew had once treated her like his daughter.

"Go!" Saw shouted, insisting even harder. This was his final wish, and he wanted nothing more than for her to grant it.

Cassian could see she wanted to argue with Saw, but the entire place was about to come down around their ears. It wasn't like they could throw a grown man in armor over their shoulders and still escape. "There's no time!"

Finally, Jyn relented and followed Cassian. As they left the chamber, Saw roared after them one final request.

"Save the Rebellion! Save the dream!"

CHAPTER 20

JYN KNEW what was happening, even if she didn't want to believe it. It couldn't be any coincidence that she'd learned about her father's work on the Death Star just before all of Jedha felt like it was about to come apart.

She hated leaving Saw behind like that, knowing she would never see him again. She'd noticed how weak and sick he was already. He hadn't had many days before him anyhow. But it saddened her to know the Empire was about to kill him.

Worse yet, if she didn't move faster, it was about to kill her, too.

Jyn didn't know the layout of Saw's hideout well enough to decide which way to run. Fortunately, Cassian seemed to have a better sense of things.

She chased him through the place's empty corridors. Everyone else—all the other prisoners and even the rest of Saw's rebels—seemed to have left already. They'd been able to see what was about to happen to Jedha, and they hadn't been worried about leaving a father figure to die.

They emerged from the monastery on a wide ledge that fronted the place, from which they should have had a spectacular view of Jedha City. Instead of the Star Destroyer that had been hovering over the Holy City, Jyn saw a massive battle station that resembled a large moon with a dish-shaped crater cut out of it.

Jedha City itself had disappeared. A cloud of ash and debris rose where the ancient city had once stood.

Cassian pushed through the people standing on the ledge, and Jyn followed him. They came up behind a man in an Imperial pilot's uniform, who had to be the prisoner they'd gone to Jedha to find.

Cassian didn't even stop as he charged past the man. All he did was shout, "Move!"

The monk and the soldier fell in behind the pilot, and all five of them ran as fast as they could. They followed Cassian to an open spot far along the ledge, away from the rest of the rebels. Those poor souls could do nothing but gape at the wave of destruction billowing out from where Jedha City had once stood and wait for their doom.

Jyn wasn't sure if Cassian had a better plan. They couldn't outrun utter destruction like that.

When they reached the end of the ledge, though, the U-wing they'd flown to Jedha came banking in hard for a pinpoint landing. Jyn spotted K-2SO at the controls. She'd never been so happy to see an Imperial security droid.

Dust flew everywhere as the ship's ramp lowered for them, and the five desperate people clambered aboard. Cassian dove for the cockpit as the U-wing's door slammed shut behind them.

"Get us out of here," he ordered the droid. "Punch it!"

K-2SO didn't need the encouragement. He'd already begun taking the U-wing back into the sky, and he swung it around to face away from the oncoming shockwave of doom.

The ledge the ship had been on gave way beneath it, crumbling into rubble. The starship struggled to compensate for the sudden change, as well as the hail of debris raining sideways.

Somewhere down there, Saw Gerrera stared up at the apocalypse that had come to Jedha and breathed his last. Jyn didn't have time to mourn him at that moment. She was too busy worrying about her own survival.

The U-wing climbed higher into the air, but not as fast as it needed to. K-2SO had reached them too late.

"Look!" the Imperial pilot shouted.

Jyn wondered why he felt the need to say something like that. They all saw what was coming at them. How could anyone look away?

The blast wave had finally peaked, and now it was crashing down on top of them. From the speed at which it moved and the angle at which it raced toward them, Jyn could see they had no chance to avoid it. In a matter of seconds, it would crush them into the rocks far below.

Cassian wasn't ready to give up. Instead, he did the unimaginable. He grabbed the lever that would thrust the U-wing into hyperspace, and he hauled back on it.

As an occasional pilot herself, Jyn knew one of the basic rules of interstellar travel was never to enter hyperspace without letting the computer make the incredibly intricate and important calculations for your route first. It was too easy to find yourself inside a planet or to pass through a star, and that was bound to put a quick end to your trip.

Since the only alternative at the moment, though, was being smashed to pieces by the fallout from the Death Star's destruction of Jedha City, she didn't see any reason not to try. She did the only thing she could think of as the scene outside the U-wing's front viewport went from dust and rocks to distorted star trails fanning out around the ship.

She held her breath and hoped.

CHAPTER 21

KRENNIC GRANTED himself permission to enjoy a wide, hungry smile as the destruction of Jedha City blossomed beneath him. The view from the overbridge of the Death Star was breathtaking. A part of him reveled in the destruction and wondered if that was how he would have felt witnessing the dawn of the universe.

The weapon he had created would alter the course of the galaxy. It would crush the Rebel Alliance and put an end to its uprising in an instant. It would bring peace to the galaxy by eliminating any question of who wielded the ultimate power.

To top it all off, Krennic got to bask in the look of astonishment that had washed over Grand Moff Tarkin's face. This would establish which of them was most deserving of the Emperor's favor, once and for all.

Tarkin turned to Krennic, his head bowed for a moment. "I believe I owe you an apology, Director Krennic. Your work exceeds all expectations."

Krennic resisted the impulse to rub Tarkin's nose in that statement. Instead, he savored it for as long as he could. Finally, all his hard work—all the horrible things he'd had to do along the way—had paid off. No one could refuse to acknowledge what he had accomplished.

"And you'll tell the Emperor as much?" Krennic almost laughed at his own comment. Of course Tarkin would. How could he possibly deny the Death Star's power?

Tarkin gave him a grave nod. "I will tell him his patience

with your misadventures has been rewarded with a weapon that will bring a swift end to the Rebellion."

Krennic couldn't help gloating a bit at that. If there was a note of reservation in Tarkin's voice, Krennic was too aglow with his success to hear it. "And that was only an inkling of the destructive potential."

They'd only used a single reactor for the test shot, and it had instantly wiped out Jedha City. Just imagine what the Death Star could do when operating at its full capacity.

Then Tarkin dropped the bombshell that Krennic knew he should have seen coming. "I will tell him that I will be taking over control of the weapon I first spoke of years ago. Effective immediately."

Krennic's face flushed. He couldn't believe the man's naked grab for power—and only moments after Krennic's amazing triumph!

"We are standing here amidst *my* achievement—not yours!"

Tarkin gave Krennic the kind of rueful look a teacher might reserve for a promising but misguided student. "I'm afraid these recent security breaches have laid bare your inadequacies as a military director."

Krennic bristled at the accusation. He had thousands of people under his purview. How could he possibly ensure that none of them would betray the Empire? He'd done everything within his power to keep as tight a lid on the security around the Death Star as possible—up to and including permanently silencing many of the outside contractors who had worked on it.

"The breaches have been filled!" Krennic protested. He stabbed a finger toward the destruction on the moon below. "Jedha has been silenced."

What more could anyone do than that?

But Krennic had underestimated Tarkin. It had never been about Krennic or his so-called inadequacies. It had been about Tarkin's carefully amassing as much power for himself as possible. He didn't care what an amazing job Krennic had done. He'd only been waiting for him to prove the Death Star was a success.

He was going to take it from him either way.

"You think this pilot acted alone?" Tarkin chuckled, making sure to rub it in. "He was dispatched from the installation on Eadu. Galen Erso's facility."

It wasn't enough for Tarkin to strip Krennic of his triumph. He wanted to make sure it hurt, too.

Krennic wasn't about to let Tarkin get away with this. If Eadu was the source of his troubles, then he would go there and pull them out by the roots. Nothing would escape his scrutiny or his wrath.

Nothing would keep him from triumph. Not Tarkin, and certainly not any traitors.

"We'll see about this," he said as he stormed off the overbridge of what he still thought of—and would always think of—as *his* Death Star.

CHAPTER 22

THE MOMENT they were clear into hyperspace and he knew they were no longer in immediate danger, Cassian sent a coded message to General Draven in the Rebellion's command center on Yavin 4. The Alliance needed to know immediately what had happened, and Cassian needed guidance on what his next step should be.

He wrote: *Weapon confirmed. Jedha destroyed. Mission target located on Eadu. Please advise.*

Cassian took great care to make sure no one else saw him sending the message. They wouldn't have been able to read the code anyway, but the fact he was using a code of any kind might send the wrong signals to the others on the U-wing.

Especially Jyn.

Cassian didn't want to have to assassinate Jyn's father. In an ideal galaxy, they'd do exactly what the council had explained to Jyn when they'd proposed the mission: find Galen Erso and bring him back alive.

With the fate of the galaxy at stake, though, Cassian understood why General Draven didn't feel like he had the luxury of taking any chances with Galen. The destruction of Jedha City had put a fine point on that.

He turned in his seat to glance at the others. The destruction of Jedha City had traumatized each of them in their own way. Bodhi was fighting the shakes and failing badly. Jyn sat there like a rock.

Baze just scowled like he'd always expected this sort of

horror to be visited on his homeworld. Chirrut kept shaking his head back and forth like he couldn't believe it.

"Baze, tell me," Chirrut said. "All of it? The whole city?"

Unlike the rest of them, the blind monk hadn't watched the Death Star blast Jedha City to pieces. No one who had seen that could doubt there was nothing of the Holy City left, but the man needed his friend to confirm it for him.

"*Tell me*," he said again.

Baze didn't say anything to soften the blow. He simply replied, "All of it."

The response from General Draven came soon enough. Once Cassian decoded it, it read: *Orders still stand. Proceed with haste, and keep to the plan.*

Cassian understood what that meant. He was to kill Galen Erso while he still had the chance.

He wasn't sure he agreed with that assessment any longer. After all, if the Death Star was already up and running, what good would killing Galen do? He would probably be more valuable to them alive.

But Cassian had his orders. He turned to K-2SO and said, "Set course for Eadu."

That got Jyn's attention. "Is that where my father is?"

Cassian nodded. "I think so."

He braced himself for a slew of uncomfortable questions. He'd spent much of his adult life as a spy. He was used to lying to people he didn't care about at all. He found it a challenge to keep quiet with Jyn about something so big as his orders to murder her father.

Before she could open her mouth again, the Imperial cargo pilot perked up and spoke to her. "You're Galen's daughter?"

She turned in her seat to peer at him. "You know him?"

Bodhi gave her a nervous nod and spoke too fast, like he couldn't stop the words from spilling out. "He said I could get right by myself. He said I could make it right if I was brave enough. And listened to what was in my heart. Do something about it."

He frowned deeply at the memory of what had just happened to Jedha City. "Guess it was too late."

Jyn shook her head. "It wasn't too late."

Baze snorted at that. He and Chirrut had lost just about everyone they knew. "Seems pretty late to me."

Jyn gave the soldier an emphatic shake of her head. "*No*," she said. "We can beat the people who did this. We can stop them."

That was the most hopeful thing Cassian had ever heard from her mouth. Actually, the most hopeful thing he'd heard in a long time. He and everyone else in the starship gave her their full attention.

"My father's message. I've seen it. They call it the Death Star, but they have no idea . . . There's a way to defeat it."

She focused on Cassian now, and he had to fight the urge to squirm beneath her glare.

"You're wrong about my father."

Did she suspect what his true orders were? He'd been careful not to let anything slip, but she clearly had suspicions. Would that change how he handled it?

"He *did* build it," Cassian pointed out.

"Because he knew they'd do it without him." The message had affected her, Cassian saw. Until now, she'd been ambivalent about the Empire and the Rebellion, only along for the ride because she had no choice. Whatever her father had said to her had sparked a fire in her eyes.

"My father made a choice," she said. "He sacrificed himself for the Rebellion. He's rigged a trap inside the weapon."

She turned to Bodhi. "That's why he sent you. To bring that message."

"Where is it?" Cassian said. "Where's the message?"

Jyn hesitated, and Cassian knew she didn't have the right answer for him. Not the one he needed.

"It was a hologram."

That was beside the point. He wanted to see the message himself. To look the man in the eye and evaluate his character.

On top of that, he needed to analyze it. Who knew what kinds of secrets Galen might have slipped into his recording? Things that Jyn couldn't possibly have known about?

"You have that message, right?"

Jyn's face fell. "Everything happened so fast. But I've just seen it!"

Cassian sympathized with her. He was the one who'd dragged her out of Saw's headquarters. From the projector where she'd been watching the hologram, he now realized.

He turned to Bodhi. "Did you see it?"

The Imperial defector shook his head like he was terrified of disappointing anyone. At least Cassian knew he was telling the truth.

"You don't believe me," Jyn said, the fact dawning on her.

Cassian frowned hard. "I'm not the one you've got to convince."

"I believe her," Chirrut said.

"That's good to know," Cassian said, not caring if the monk heard the sarcasm in his voice.

"What kind of trap?" Baze asked Jyn. "You said your father made a trap."

"The reactor." Jyn seemed relieved to be able to talk about the message with anyone besides Cassian. "He's placed a weakness there. He's been hiding it for years. He said if you can blow the reactor—the module—the whole system goes down."

Having spilled all that, she turned back to Cassian. "You need to send word to the Alliance."

"I've done that."

She narrowed her eyes at him. She knew he couldn't have relayed the latest information that fast.

"They have to know there's a way to destroy this thing! They have to go to Scarif and get the plans."

Cassian shook his head. "I can't risk sending that. We're in the heart of Imperial territory."

It may have sounded like a lie to her, but he was telling the truth. He didn't trust the Rebellion's coding system. It was fine for sending oblique messages like he and Draven had traded, but when it came to something that had to be specific, he wouldn't dare use it.

Jyn considered him for a long moment as she set her jaw in determination. She'd gotten this close to her father, and Cassian could see she wasn't about to give up now.

"Then we'll find him—and bring him back. And he can tell them himself!"

Cassian gave her an *all right* nod. Those were her orders, after all.

Unfortunately, they weren't *his* orders.

CHAPTER 23

BODHI ROOK couldn't remember a time he'd been so terrified, and the past few days had been filled with all sorts of nerve-racking things. He'd escaped from the Empire with a secret message from Galen Erso, one of the top scientists in the galaxy. He'd delivered the message to Saw Gerrera—and been tortured for it.

Maybe he'd been more scared when Bor Gullet had ripped his mind to pieces to make sure he wasn't lying, but truth be told, Bodhi couldn't remember most of it. He was grateful for that. He wasn't sure he was entirely over the effects, but he was eager to put the experience behind him either way.

Through most of that, though, he'd held his fate in his own hands. Now, as a pilot himself, he had to watch a rebel and a reprogrammed Imperial security droid try to land a U-wing in a horrifying storm that took them through a series of gigantic rock formations that seemed to stab at them from out of nowhere.

He couldn't help coaching from behind. He understood why they didn't yet trust him to fly the ship, but he wondered if he should have insisted on taking the controls anyhow.

Did they think he planned to crash the ship into one of those spires, killing them all at once? He was desperate to make up for having worked for the Empire for so long, not suicidal.

"Go low!" Bodhi shouted at them. "Lower!"

The crazy droid argued with him. "This ship was not meant to be flown this way."

At least he bothered to respond that time. Bodhi brought down his tone. "They have landing trackers. They have patrol squadrons. You've got to stay in the canyon. Keep it low."

Otherwise, the Empire was sure to spot them, and then their little trip to Eadu would end fast—and probably in a big ball of fire.

"Watch the right!" Cassian shouted at the droid.

For a machine that supposedly had lightning-fast reflexes, the droid was *not* making Bodhi feel good about his flying skills. He wondered if it was too late to try to take the controls away.

Right then they hit an air pocket and dropped hard enough to lift Bodhi out of his seat. He gave up sitting and tried crouching behind them instead.

The droid didn't seem bothered, but he did update their odds. "There is a twenty-six percent chance of failure."

Cassian glanced back at Bodhi. "How much farther?"

Bodhi gave him a frustrated shrug. "I don't know—I'm not sure. I never really come this way." And why would he? As an Imperial cargo pilot, he'd always had clearance in the past. He hadn't had any reason to risk his life this way—until now.

"We're close," he said anyhow. "We're close—I know that."

"Now there's a thirty-five percent chance of failure."

Bodhi felt like smacking K-2SO in the back of his metal head, but Cassian shouted the droid down first.

"I don't want to know! Thank you."

"I understand," the droid said. Bodhi wasn't sure he really did though.

He tried to ignore the droid and kept his attention focused on the U-wing's viewport instead. The rocks seemed familiar, although he'd never seen any of them from that angle before.

He knew they were getting close, but exactly how close were they?

Too close!

"Now! Put it down now!"

"The wind—" The droid started to protest, but Bodhi wasn't having any of it.

"If you keep going, you'll be right over the shuttle depot!"

Bodhi hoped he didn't have to describe exactly how much that would be a *bad thing*. If anyone in the shuttle depot spotted the U-wing, they'd instantly raise the alarm. The six of them didn't have a chance of taking on an entire Imperial base.

The lights of the shuttle depot speared up through the rain, as if to prove Bodhi right. K-2SO recognized the threat they posed and swung the ship into a hard turn.

The side of the U-wing clipped a column of rock as the droid brought it back. The impact jolted the entire ship and threw Bodhi off his feet.

He floundered about for a handhold as the ship fell into a steep dive. He couldn't tell if K-2SO still had control of it or if they were all about to die.

"Hold on tight!" Cassian shouted. "We're coming down hard!"

Bodhi wanted to snap off a sarcastic reply to that announcement of the obvious, but he couldn't catch enough breath to manage it. Then he ran out of time.

The starship smacked into the ground, and Bodhi did the same to the ship's floor. From the sound of it, one of the struts on the landing gear failed on impact, and from the way the ship angled forward onto its nose, it was the one up front.

Bodhi had seen starships crash like that before.

Sometimes—if there was a friendly port nearby with a fast and resourceful team of mechanics—the ship might be made space worthy again.

But they were essentially rebels stuck behind Imperial lines. No help was on the way.

Bodhi was more scared than ever.

CHAPTER 24

CASSIAN WANTED to kick the U-wing into pieces. He'd gone outside to inspect the ship in the violent storm and darkness, by himself, and he hadn't liked a single thing he'd seen. The landing—if he could call it that—had smashed not only the landing gear but other parts of the craft. They weren't going anywhere in it.

Now he needed to find and assassinate Galen Erso and also somehow steal a ship big enough to carry all six of them safely off the planet. If they wanted to survive, anyway. He didn't need K-2SO to tell him that the chances of Jyn trying to kill him after he murdered her father approached a hundred percent.

The only bit of good news he could find was that the storm had covered their approach so well that the Imperials in the base didn't seem to have noticed their crash at all.

The worst part, though, was that the ship's communications array had been destroyed in the crash, too. That meant Cassian couldn't call for help. He couldn't even signal General Draven that they'd made it to Eadu and found the facility where Galen Erso supposedly worked.

Because of that, Draven would probably think Cassian and his ragtag team were dead. What would he do then?

Cassian didn't know for sure, but General Draven wasn't one to sit on his hands and hope things would work out in his favor. He preferred action.

When it came down to it, Cassian had to admit he was much the same way.

He went back into the ship, and all eyes turned to him. He knew they were waiting on him for some kind of plan. He just had to come up with one that wouldn't get them all killed—at least not until he finished the mission.

"Bodhi," he said. "Where's the lab?"

"The research facility?"

Maybe he needed to give the kid a break. Saw had tortured him, after all. But he didn't have time for this right now. "*Yeah. Where is it?*"

His tone seemed to shake Bodhi awake. "It's just over the ridge."

"And that's a shuttle depot straight ahead of us? You are sure about that?"

The pilot nodded. "Yes."

As shaken as the man might be, Cassian decided to believe him.

"We'll have to hope there's still an Imperial ship left to steal. Here's what we're doing."

He glanced at each of the others to make sure they were listening. They hung on his every word.

"Hopefully the storm keeps up and keeps us hidden down here. Bodhi, you're coming with me. We'll go up the ridge and check it out."

The pilot jumped to his feet with a sharp nod. He was ready.

Jyn unfolded herself and stood next to him. "I'm coming with you."

Cassian shook her off. "No. Your father's message. We can't risk it. You're the messenger."

He realized how thin that sounded as an excuse, but he

didn't have anything better. He couldn't just say, *I can't have you around, because I might have to kill your father.*

"That's ridiculous," she responded. "We *all* got the message. Everyone here knows it."

She could obviously tell he was trying to protect her from something. Cassian could only hope she didn't guess what.

He was about to explain that none of them would remember what she said with as much clarity as she did. Then K-2SO spoke up.

"'One blast to the reactor module and the whole system goes down.' That's how you said it. 'The whole system goes down.'"

"*Get to work fixing our comms,*" Cassian snapped at the droid. He didn't know if that was even possible, but it would keep K-2SO out of trouble for a little while at least.

Cassian turned back to Jyn and tried to seem casual. "All I want to do right now is get a handle on what we're up against."

He'd lied to so many people over the years. Why did he have trouble lying to her? Maybe it was because she was on his side now and he didn't want to betray her.

He turned to Bodhi. "So we're gonna go very small and very careful up the rise and see what's what. Let's get out of here."

Jyn crossed her arms and frowned at him, still suspicious, but she didn't object. *I'll take that,* Cassian thought. *At least for now.*

Bodhi followed him out into the storm, and Cassian cast about for which way to go. He spotted a route that led lower and one that climbed higher. He started for the lower one, but Bodhi stopped him.

"No, no. We've gotta go up."

Bodhi led the way from there, and Cassian followed.

CHAPTER 25

JYN HAD almost started to like Cassian. He'd done well in Jedha City. She could see why the Rebellion had sent him along with her on the mission, as dangerous as it was. He could handle just about anything thrown at him, and she respected that.

On the trip out to Eadu, though, he'd started to clam up. And when he'd insisted on leaving the rest of them in the crashed ship while he and Bodhi scouted the place? That hadn't sat right with her.

The storm raged outside the ship, and Jyn was happy to have an excuse not to go out into it. She didn't like the idea of running into a patrol of stormtroopers in that mess, either.

But Cassian hadn't given her a *good* excuse, and she knew it.

Chirrut spoke up. "Does he look like a killer?"

For a moment, Jyn wasn't sure if the monk was talking to her or someone else. Either way, Baze answered first.

"No. He has the face of a friend."

That still mystified her. The two men had the way about them of longtime friends who shared so much background they didn't need to explain much to each other, but she wasn't in on that with them.

"Who are you talking about?" she asked.

Baze nodded at the door. "Captain Andor."

Cassian? Had the two noticed something about him that she hadn't?

"Why do you ask that?"

Baze shrugged. He hadn't asked anything.

Jyn focused on Chirrut and spoke directly to him. "What do you mean, 'Does he look like a killer?'"

"The Force moves darkly near a creature that's about to kill."

What did that mean? Jyn wasn't inclined to give too much credence to a monk babbling about a failed religion. Cassian had said he and Bodhi were going out to scout the area. If he was planning to kill someone, would he have taken Bodhi with him?

K-2SO spoke then, making an offhand observation as he continued his work. "His weapon *was* in the sniper configuration."

The droid had a horrible habit of speaking his mind without a filter of any sort. Perhaps this was one time when it would work to Jyn's advantage.

Jyn didn't know what Cassian was up to. She didn't have any real proof he had gone out there to kill someone. Like her father.

But this wasn't a court of law. She didn't need proof. The one thing she did need, she realized, was to find out—before it was too late.

Without a word, Jyn headed for the U-wing's door. She slipped into the rain-soaked night.

She wasn't sure where Cassian and Bodhi were headed, but they weren't loitering near the ship for sure. She picked a likely direction and started off into the darkness.

Soon Jyn came to a fork in the path she'd chosen, one way leading up and the other down. The way down looked like it offered her a better chance to actually get into the base, so she chose that.

CHAPTER 26

BAZE WATCHED Jyn leave the U-wing, and he frowned in disapproval. He'd been in situations like this before with a group of soldiers, all on the edge. They needed to work together—to act like a team—if they wanted to survive, but instead the people who were supposedly leading their trip seemed set on keeping the rest of them in the dark.

He felt too sad to care much about it though. Instead, his thoughts kept returning to his poor, dear, absolutely destroyed Jedha.

He had been born and raised there, and no matter how far he might have wandered from it at times, it had always been the center of his universe. Everyone he'd grown up with. The priests. The Temple.

Gone. All of it.

The only exception was Chirrut.

True, Chirrut was his oldest and best friend. The two shared a bond that nothing else in their lives had managed to fracture. Somehow, it had even survived the destruction of their homeland.

But now where was their home? Where did they belong? And—most important, Baze thought—what could they do to take revenge on the monsters who had murdered so many?

Baze had been so tangled in his own thoughts, he almost hadn't seen Chirrut head for the ship's exit. He realized that Chirrut had given Jyn enough of a head start that she'd probably be long gone, and then he'd gotten up and made to leave the ship too.

As far as Baze was concerned, though, Chirrut wasn't going anywhere without him—certainly not out into that storm. He pushed himself to his feet and padded after his friend.

When they emerged from the U-wing, Baze glanced around to make sure Jyn was in fact gone. Chirrut didn't seem concerned about that at all. He simply went out into the rain, tapping his stick on the unfamiliar ground before him. Perhaps he could feel her tracks that way. It wouldn't have surprised Baze.

"Where are you going?" Baze asked Chirrut. It was insane for a blind man to wander around in storm-swept mountains on the outskirts of an Imperial base, and they both knew it.

"I'm going to follow Jyn," Chirrut said. "Her path is clear."

Baze supposed he understood that choice. The woman had the mission she'd announced to them all, and she had set out to do it. About Cassian, Baze wasn't so sure.

"Alone?" Baze said. "Good luck."

He didn't want to do this. Let Jyn and Cassian and the Imperial pilot wander around and get lost in the rain. Let them betray each other. Baze just wanted to stay dry and plot his revenge.

"I don't need luck," Chirrut said. "I have you."

Baze grimaced at his friend. He knew he couldn't let Chirrut take off from the ship on his own. The man had called Baze's bluff. He had no choice but to follow him, like it or not.

CHAPTER 27

BODHI DIDN'T like this at all, and it wasn't just because Cassian had dragged him out into the rain after he and his maybe faulty droid had nearly killed everyone in that terrible excuse for a landing. If they were just scouting around to make sure no Imperials had spotted them, they could have managed it with a quick trip around their crash site. Instead, Cassian had decided it was perfect weather for a little mountain climbing.

Bodhi soon realized that Cassian had other ambitions for their hike. They kept making their way up, up, up until they reached the top of the ridge that separated them from the Imperial base.

Once they topped the crest, Bodhi and Cassian couldn't miss the secret base. Most of the base lay buried behind the face of the cliff across the valley from the two men, but the Empire still needed to let shuttles in and out of the place. The Empire had lit its landing platform with spotlights to make it easier for legitimate shuttle pilots—like Bodhi had once been—to find it.

Cassian pulled Bodhi down next to him, as if anyone in the base could spot them all the way over there. In the storm. At night.

But Bodhi went along with it anyhow. Cassian was the spy, after all.

Cassian pulled out a set of quadnocs and focused them on

the landing platform. Bodhi didn't think there would be much out there to look at, but he decided to let the spy go spy if he wanted to.

Then a squad of stormtroopers marched out onto the platform.

That wasn't the standard procedure, Bodhi knew. The many times he'd flown cargo there, he'd only had a few of the white-armored soldiers come out to meet him. Most of the time, they ignored him entirely, and he did the same to them.

Cassian handed the quadnocs to Bodhi. "You see Erso out there?"

Bodhi almost started to explain that Erso wasn't a storm-trooper, but he realized Cassian probably knew that. He took the quadnocs and zoomed in on the people on the landing platform instead.

The only people out there were the stormtroopers. Bodhi expected them to be squirming in their armor, unhappy to be out in that weather, but they all stood at perfect atten-tion, almost like they were expecting an inspection. Then he saw why.

More stormtroopers appeared, and they were escorting the project engineers onto the platform. The engineers seemed less thrilled than the stormtroopers, as they didn't have any armor to protect them from the weather.

And Galen Erso stood among them.

This had to be huge. It was one thing to see the engineers get lined up outside like this in the middle of a storm, but for Galen to join them?

Bodhi handed the quadnocs back to Cassian. "That's *him*! That's him—Galen—in the dark suit."

He pointed toward where Galen stood, and Cassian trained the quadnocs on the man. His face grew grim.

Bodhi felt strange spying on the man who'd sent him off with a message for Jyn not so long before. Now that they'd found him, what were they going to do?

A loud noise came roaring up behind them, and Bodhi instantly recognized it as the exhaust of an Imperial shuttle. He turned around to gape at it as it zoomed toward them, and he didn't even realize he'd stood up as he did it.

Cassian grabbed Bodhi and hauled him back down just as the shuttle scudded overhead on its way to the landing platform. If anyone inside it—or in the base—had seen him, they didn't show it.

Cassian motioned down the path they'd followed to the top of the ridge. "Get back down there and find us a ride out of here."

That made sense, Bodhi thought. The U-wing was never going to fly again—not for them, at least. If they wanted to leave Eadu, they were going to need another ship.

Bodhi had just the one in mind.

Before he turned to go, though, he saw Cassian ready his rifle and start fiddling with the scope.

"What're you doing?" Bodhi asked.

"You heard me."

Was Cassian going to start shooting already? Before Bodhi even had a chance to snag them a new ride? The pilot wasn't comfortable with that.

"You said we came up here just to have a look."

"I'm here. I'm looking. Go."

Bodhi frowned. Cassian was the spy, sure, and it was his operation. But something didn't seem right.

Either way, they still needed that ship. Bodhi started back down the way they'd come.

"Hurry!" Cassian barked.

Bodhi kicked it into high gear. No matter what Cassian was about to do, he wanted his hands on a shuttle—and fast.

CHAPTER 28

KRENNIC WAS in a rage the entire trip to Eadu. Tarkin had stripped him of control of the Death Star, and worse yet, he'd laid the blame for that at Krennic's feet!

The idea that it had been his own fault gnawed at Krennic. True, the renegade pilot who'd defected to the Rebellion— a man by the name of Rook, he thought—had done so under his watch, but he couldn't be expected to keep track of everyone who worked on the Death Star. But according to Tarkin's jabs, Rook's betrayal didn't encompass the full extent of the problem.

Although Krennic had dismissed that idea at first, the more he thought about it, the more he knew it had to be true. After all, how could a single pilot's treachery cause any potential damage to the Death Star?

But this Rook, he reportedly had information about the Death Star that could be used against it. Krennic had no idea what it could be, but he suspected that Tarkin had been right about the source of it. The problems all had to stem from the base on Eadu.

That made him more furious with Tarkin than ever. It wasn't enough the man was stealing his triumph; he actually managed to be right about the seeds of his downfall, too!

Krennic didn't know if it would do him any good personally, but he planned to find the traitors and root them out. Permanently.

By the time his shuttle landed on Eadu, the entire base had

been alerted to his arrival. A platoon of the research facility's best stormtroopers stood on the landing platform, ready to greet him, along with the place's top Imperial officials.

Krennic let them stand there in the rain for a bit longer than necessary, just to show them who was in charge.

There was no Tarkin present, no Emperor, no Darth Vader. When it came to this facility, *he* ruled.

He emerged from his ship into the chilly, rainy night, his death troopers alongside him. Galen Erso stood at the front of the group of officials, and he stepped forward to greet Krennic like the old friend he was. None of the others had the spine to manage it.

"Well, Galen," Krennic said. "The battle station is complete. You must be very proud."

"Proud as I can be, Krennic."

Galen didn't seem that happy, but then he never had smiled all that much. Not since Krennic had been forced to bring him back from Lah'mu. Krennic supposed that losing his wife and child could do that to a man, but Galen had adapted in the best possible way, throwing himself into the challenge of their work and hammering away at it until he succeeded.

"Gather your engineers," Krennic told Galen. "I have an announcement to make."

Let them think he'd come to praise them for the effectiveness of the weapons testing he'd overseen at Jedha. That would bring them up faster.

Galen went to relay the order to his underlings. Moments later, his entire team joined them on the platform. Some of the people squinted at the wind and rain as if they hadn't breathed fresh air in a long time.

"Is that all of them?" Krennic asked.

"Yes," Galen said, gesturing to the people standing in their white-and-blue jumpsuits.

Krennic stepped before the engineers and gathered them all together beneath his steely glare. There was only one way to deal with the kind of treachery he'd discovered: sheer and utter ruthlessness.

"Gentlemen. One of you betrayed the Empire. One of you conspired with a pilot to send messages to the Rebellion. And I urge that traitor to step forward."

The sniveling weaklings glanced at each other. None of them wanted to own up to it. Among them, they couldn't even find one person to pin it on.

Krennic waited longer than he felt necessary. Even in his thirst for justice, he could be charitable, he thought.

"Very well. I'll consider it a group effort then."

At his signal, his death troopers raised their weapons. There were no traitors among them, at least. They pointed their rifles straight at the line of engineers.

If that didn't get them to crack, Krennic believed nothing would. Then he'd be forced to have them all executed. Until now, he might have hesitated to give such an order for fear of destroying a team he very much needed, but with the Death Star operational—and Tarkin having stolen it from him any-way—he didn't see the harm.

Krennic raised his hand to signal his death troopers to pre-pare themselves. "Ready . . . aim . . . and . . ."

Just before Krennic brought down his arm and said "fire," Galen leaped forward to intervene.

"Stop, stop, *stop!*" he said. "Krennic, stop!"

Krennic did as requested, although his death troopers did

not stand down. Galen quickly went on to explain. "It was me! It was me. They have nothing to do with it. Spare them."

Galen slumped forward, the fight all gone out of him. The man hadn't even been facing execution, but he was willing to let the full extent of Krennic's wrath land on him if it would save his people.

He'd always been a fool.

Krennic beckoned for Galen to come toward him, well out of the line of fire. Galen shuffled over, ready to suffer whatever punishment might be handed down to him.

Krennic looked to the engineers again. They were awash with relief that Galen would take the fall for them. They were too surprised—too unsure about what was happening—to thank him for his sacrifice.

Krennic stared at them, despising them all. He said one word. "Fire."

The death troopers lit up the night with their rifles, and each and every one of the engineers collapsed, dead before they hit the platform.

CHAPTER 29

CASSIAN STARED in horror and frustration as the death troopers gunned down the engineers. For the past several minutes, he'd been watching the entire scene play out through the scope on his rifle, waiting for a clear shot at Galen Erso. He'd gotten one just a moment before, but he'd balked at taking it.

He didn't know what had stayed his hand. He'd killed many people before, all in the name of the Rebellion. If blasting away one man would save millions of lives, the answer seemed clear.

But it wasn't, and Cassian knew it. Galen had already completed his work on the Death Star. Killing him now wouldn't stop the Empire from using the battle station again.

On top of that, Cassian had watched Galen try to sacrifice himself for the other people on his engineering team. He didn't know how he could shoot a man right after witnessing such a selfless act.

There was also the fact that the man was Jyn's long-lost father. Killing him would shatter her, he knew. They might have been apart for years, but she still loved him. Cassian could see it in her eyes every time the man's name came up.

Cassian grabbed his quadnocs again and zoomed in on the slaughter happening on the landing platform. Galen stood there gawking at the death of his compatriots. As the last one fell, he turned toward Krennic, who backhanded him across the jaw.

Galen fell to his knees, holding his hand to his injured face.

Cassian lowered his quadnocs, and as he did, he spotted Jyn. She was just beneath the edge of the landing platform, climbing onto it from below, but she didn't seem to notice the stormtrooper wandering toward her.

He didn't know what he could do to help her. If the stormtrooper spotted her, she was done for. If Cassian shot the stormtrooper, the blast would draw attention to Jyn, as well.

The stormtrooper moved closer to the edge of the platform and stared out into the rain. All it would take was for him to glance down, and he'd spot Jyn in an instant. Then he'd take the rifle he was carelessly toting around and shoot her dead.

Jyn saw the stormtrooper. Rather than crawl back and try to hide, though, she reached up and grabbed the end of the stormtrooper's rifle. Then she hauled backward with all her weight and pulled the man out and over the edge.

The stormtrooper disappeared, flailing, into the stormy darkness. If he cried out, no one seemed to notice. Perhaps they were too busy listening to Galen's anguish.

Right then, Cassian's comlink came on, and K-2SO spoke. "Cassian!" the droid said. "Cassian, can you hear me?"

Cassian grabbed his comlink. If the stormtroopers couldn't hear their friend fall to his death, then they weren't going to be able to hear Cassian speaking into the comm from so much farther away.

"I'm here," Cassian said. "You got it working."

"Affirmative," the droid said. "But we have a problem. There's an Alliance squadron approaching. Clear the area!"

Cassian almost dropped his comm. He glanced down to see Jyn still under the platform. She was creeping around to where she could climb up on it and not be seen.

"No, no, no, no!" he said into the comlink. "Tell them to hold up! Jyn's on that platform!"

Cassian grimaced. He knew how these kinds of attacks went. The squadron would maintain radio silence after a certain point. They didn't want the Empire to know they were coming, after all.

No matter who might be trying to shout at them to stop—from General Draven on down—it might already be too late.

CHAPTER 30

KRENNIC GLARED down at Galen, whom he'd knocked to his knees. The man might have been one of the most brilliant minds Krennic had ever encountered, but he was lousy in a fight.

He could barely believe Galen had been the one to betray him. To have stayed quiet for so long, silently working against him—against the Empire? He hadn't thought the scientist had such doggedness in him.

Krennic saw now that he must have been wrong. Anyone who could work so long and hard to help him figure out how to power the Death Star with kyber crystals had more than enough determination to do whatever he wanted.

And of course, Krennic had given him the motivation, hadn't he?

If only Lyra hadn't been so stubborn. She'd been the one to lure Galen away from his work in the first place. Then she'd gone and trained her blaster on Krennic in an effort to make him leave her family alone.

What choice had he had at that point but to execute her?

That's what had put them on this road. If Lyra had only been willing to go along with Krennic's plans, she'd still be alive, and Galen would have been happily solving the problems with the Death Star. They might even have finished work on it years before.

Now that he knew Galen for who he really was though—a traitor to both the Empire and their friendship—Krennic wanted him to pay for his crimes. He wanted to make the man hurt.

"I fired your weapon," Krennic told Galen. "Jedha. Saw Gerrera. His band of fanatics. The Holy City. The last reminder of the Jedi. An entire planet will be next."

Galen set his bruised jaw and stared up at Krennic with defiance. Had the man ever had that kind of passion before, or had Krennic just never noticed?

"You'll never win," Galen said.

Krennic couldn't help smirking at that. "Now, where have I heard that before?"

Lyra had said the same thing just before he'd had her killed. Galen could hardly think he was about to fare any better.

An alarm began to blare then, and it took Krennic a moment to figure out what it was for. They used different patterns for different troubles. This particular alarm was reserved to warn people about an imminent air attack.

Krennic looked up at the sky. Was this a drill? If so, it was a terribly timed one.

He got his answer when the first X-wing appeared out of the storm clouds and opened fire on the landing platform. The first salvo stitched blasts across the platform, sending stormtroopers and the bodies of the dead engineers flying.

Krennic, though, remained unharmed. If the rebels planned to try their luck with him there, they were going to pay for their audacity.

"Return fire!" Krennic barked at his death troopers. To the rest of the stormtroopers and officers, he shouted, "To your stations! Get our fighters in the air! *Now!*"

More laser fire rained down as an entire squadron of X-wings zoomed overhead, strafing the platform as they went.

Then it grew quiet, but Krennic knew it would only be for a moment. They would be swinging around for another pass for sure.

Smoke billowed across the platform, obscuring Krennic's view. For a moment, Krennic wasn't sure which way he should move. He hoped the smoke would at least keep the X-wing pilots from seeing him when they came around again.

He saw Galen stagger to his feet, and he considered shooting the man dead right there to keep the rebels from robbing him of his revenge.

Despite that, he was more concerned about his own skin. He was about to race inside to take cover when a woman appeared out of the swirling clouds. She was young, with blazing hazel eyes and tied-back dark hair, and she seemed entirely out of place.

She wasn't a stormtrooper or an Imperial officer, and she wasn't wearing one of the jumpsuits the engineers favored. In fact, she looked dirty, tired, and more than a little desperate. As she approached, she shouted a single word.

"Father!"

Galen spun around to see who could have said that word and who she was talking to. As he did, the woman raised a blaster pistol and leveled it at Krennic. For a moment, he thought he might die without any idea who his killer was.

Then a Y-wing roared in low and let loose a proton torpedo that blasted the landing platform apart.

CHAPTER 31

JYN HADN'T been sure she'd be able to make it onto the landing platform, but the sight of her father standing there above her had pushed her to take insane risks. When the stormtrooper had wandered over to peer over the edge of the platform, she'd thought he would have seen and shot her instantly, but she struck first, bold and fast. That's why she was still breathing and he wasn't.

She'd finally managed to work her way to a secluded edge of the platform and climbed up to hide behind a shipping crate someone had left there. From that new vantage point, she spotted her father once more, and she wanted nothing more than to race over to him and reveal that she was there. She knew, though, that Krennic would have her shot on the spot. She had to wait until she had her chance.

Then the X-wings appeared in the sky. Crazy as it was, she decided that was her time. If Krennic managed to survive the attack, he'd have her father executed for sure, just as he'd done with those innocent engineers. The confusion and terror—and smoke!—the attack produced gave her cover, and she meant to use it.

She vowed to herself that Krennic would not steal her father away again, as he had years before, back on Lah'mu. She called out to Galen, and their eyes met.

Then the torpedo hit the platform.

The blast sent Jyn flying. Stunned, she glanced up, convinced that the X-wings had come gunning for her. Then she spotted a flight of TIE fighters racing into the air to meet them. She'd never been so happy to see Imperial pilots doing their job in her life.

Anti-aircraft turrets joined in then, blasting away at the rebels in the sky. Normally, Jyn would have wanted to take down the stormtroopers manning them as fast as she could, but they were the only thing keeping another torpedo from blasting her and her father to bits.

Her ears rang with a high-pitched whine, and for a long while, it was all she could do to try to catch her breath. As her lungs struggled with that, she spied a pair of Imperial officers racing out of the smoke. They darted straight over to Krennic and began dragging him toward his shuttle.

Overhead, a turret found its target. A wounded X-wing spun out of control and crashed somewhere in the mountains. A boom marked its passing.

Jyn saw the distinctive bolt of a lightbow shoot out from another spot in the mountains and lance straight through a TIE fighter. The spacecraft spun like a runaway top and came smashing down into the turret. Everything flared white in a massive blast that shook the platform once more.

Jyn shook her head again and again, but it didn't seem to want to start working. She could barely tell which way was up or down.

She spotted Krennic staggering up the ramp into his shuttle. He paused there for a moment, as if he wanted to go back and take on the rebel squadron himself. One of his officers grabbed him again and insisted he get on the ship.

"Director! We have to evacuate!"

Krennic glanced back toward Jyn's father and saw that he lay there unmoving. Nodding at the officer's suggestion, he turned and hustled onto the shuttle. The ramp closed behind him.

Jyn wanted to call out to her father again, but she could see he wouldn't answer her. Somehow, she hoped that he was still alive.

She struggled to her feet and steadied herself to make her way toward her father. Just as she started moving, though, the wash from Krennic's rising shuttle hit her hard.

It nearly swept her from the platform. She managed to stop herself at the last instant, and as the pressure faded, she clawed back toward where Galen lay sprawled across what was left of the platform.

He was barely alive and fading fast. She couldn't believe she'd come all this way, fought through so many years on her own, only to find him like this, in his dying moments.

She cradled him in her arms the best she could, but he showed no recognition. The light in his eyes would soon go out.

"Papa," she said. "It's Jyn."

"Jyn?" He looked up at her, trying to recognize her.

It had been so long. She'd been through so much.

She nodded down at him, tears welling in her eyes. A softness washed over his face then, and he opened his mouth to speak.

"Stardust . . ." he said. "It must be destroyed. . . ."

"I know," she said, trying to comfort him. "I've seen your message."

He tried to say something else—anything else—but he couldn't manage it. Instead, he reached up to brush the hair from her face and caress her cheek. Then his strength left him entirely, and he was gone.

Jyn stared at him, tears streaming down her face. Even

though they hadn't seen each other in years, he'd loomed so large in her life, every day. She couldn't believe he was actually dead.

"Papa?" she said. "No, no! Papa . . . Papa! Come on!"

A stormtrooper emerged from the smoke then and trained his rifle on Jyn. She saw him, but she knew there was nothing she could do to stop him. She couldn't reach her blaster—not in time.

She would die there right next to her father. The fact that it was the last thing he would have wanted made the whole situation that much worse.

A shot lanced out from another direction, though, and the blast caught the stormtrooper in the chest. As the stormtrooper fell, Jyn glanced around to see who could have possibly saved her.

Cassian charged down the platform then, straight toward her, his blaster still in his hand. "Jyn," he said as he tried to guide her away from Galen's body. "We gotta go. Come on."

She looked down at her father, and it hurt so much. "I can't leave him."

Cassian leaned in and spoke to her in short but caring words. "Listen to me. He's gone. There's nothing you can do. Come on."

Much as she hated it, she knew he was right. She extended her hand toward him. "Help me."

He hauled her to her feet and took off running back the way he'd come. She was still hurting, but she knew she had to keep up with him. Otherwise, the stormtroopers would kill them both.

"Come on!" he shouted as he dragged her along. "Move!"

CHAPTER 32

JUST BECAUSE Jyn and Cassian had made it off the landing platform didn't mean they were safe. As they raced away, a squad of stormtroopers spotted them and gave chase.

More blaster fire hailed down from above, taking down one stormtrooper after another. Jyn glanced up and spotted Baze standing on a ridge above them, grim and furious as he blasted away.

"Come on!" Cassian shouted as Jyn stole one last glance at her father. "Come on!"

Cassian led the way, shooting at more stormtroopers as they went, and Jyn followed him up a twisting path that led through a narrow canyon. Blaster fire chased them, knocking rubble from the canyon walls, which at least kept the stormtroopers from getting a clear shot.

As they rounded a turn and came into a wider area, Baze and Chirrut charged up to meet them. For a moment, Jyn was thrilled that all four of them had managed to meet up, but she realized that their U-wing was still out of commission. The best they could hope for was to find Bodhi and K-2SO holed up there and make a last stand until the stormtroopers and TIE fighters overwhelmed them.

Jyn flinched as she heard the roar of a ship approaching from the other side of the ridge. Was it a Y-wing come to blast them to pieces, thinking they were Imperials on the run? Or would it be a TIE fighter taking them down as rebel intruders?

Jyn thought she had her answer when the ship crested the

ridge and she saw it was an Imperial cargo shuttle. Her breath caught in her chest as she waited for it to open fire on her and the others.

It blasted away, but the shots all went over her head, taking out the stormtroopers chasing them instead.

Peering through the viewport, Jyn spotted Bodhi at the cargo shuttle's controls, with K-2SO beside him as his copilot. She felt tempted to cheer with relief, but she stopped herself for fear of drawing any other stormtroopers in their direction.

The cargo shuttle hauled up close and came to a hover right next to them. A ramp lowered, and Jyn heard Bodhi shouting at them. "Let's go, let's go, let's go!"

Jyn and Cassian raced aboard the ship, and Bodhi was there to greet them and help them inside. Eager to leave, K-2SO started to take off, but Cassian ordered him to stop long enough for Chirrut and Baze to get on board, too.

Once everyone was safely on the ship, Bodhi threw the switch to raise the ramp and charged back toward the cockpit. "Kay-Tu! All aboard. Let's go!"

"Copy you," the droid said. "Launching and away."

Bodhi and K-2SO kept the cargo shuttle low to avoid Imperial attention. They weaved their way through the canyons, moving away from the secret base in which Jyn's father had worked. Where his dead body now lay.

An explosion rocked the base behind them, sending a fireball up into the stormy night. The rebel squadron's attack had done its job.

Bodhi flipped a series of switches on the ship's dashboard, giving instructions to K-2SO as he went. "Ion thrusters low until we've cleared the storm."

Jyn's head was still spinning from the torpedo blast that

had killed her father. As she sat there in the bay and managed to catch her breath, she began to realize what had just happened, and she was not happy about it. In fact, the more she thought about it, the more furious she got.

"You lied to me."

All eyes in the ship turned toward her, and they could all see the righteous anger welling up in her, about to explode. Most of them were confused. One person was not.

Cassian met Jyn's gaze straight on. He'd been waiting for her to figure it out, and now he thought he could weather her storm.

"You're in shock," he said, dismissing her outrage.

"You went up there to kill my father."

It had to be true. The way he'd gone off to scout the area, refusing to let her go along. The way the rebel squadron had come in and bombed the base while her father stood there on the landing platform. They thought he'd failed at his job, and they were determined to take care of it for him.

"You don't know what you're talking about." He wouldn't look her directly in the eye.

"Deny it," she dared him. He wasn't answering her accusations, just deflecting them. She wasn't about to let him get away with it.

"You're in shock and looking for someplace to put it. I've seen it before."

Jyn worked her jaw. "I bet you have." How many people had he killed? All in the name of his beloved Rebel Alliance? The so-called greater good?

She looked to the others. K-2SO kept focused on flying the ship, but Bodhi had turned around. She could see in his eyes that he knew she was right.

Baze saw it, too. Even blind Chirrut knew.

"*They* know. You lied to me about why we came here, and you lied about why you went up alone."

Cassian scowled. At that moment, he gave up pretending he hadn't been there to kill Galen. He switched to defending himself instead.

"I had every chance to pull the trigger," he said. "But did I?" He turned to the others, hoping they would rally to his side. "*Did I?*"

They remained unmoved. Jyn lit into him again.

"You might as well have. My father was living proof, and you put him at risk! Those were Alliance bombs that killed him!"

"I had orders!" Cassian said, as if that explained everything. "Orders that I disobeyed! But you wouldn't understand that."

Jyn scoffed at him. "*Orders?* When you know they're *wrong?* You might as well be a stormtrooper."

"What do you know?"

If Cassian had been unrepentant before, he was furious now. He rounded on her, ready to have this fight out once and for all.

"We don't all have the luxury of deciding where and when we want to care about something. Suddenly the Rebellion is *real* for you? Some of us live it!

"I've been in this fight since I was six years old! You're not the only one who lost everything. Some of us just decided to do something about it!"

There it was: the real bone of contention between them. He'd lost everything as a child, too, but he'd dedicated his life to the Rebellion because of it.

She'd been a part of that at one point, back when she was

with Saw, but after the man had abandoned her, she'd cut the Rebellion out of her life. And where had that gotten her?

Right back there, fighting against the Empire anyway.

"You can't talk your way around this," she said to him in a hard, cool voice. She hated that he had a point.

He wasn't done with her yet. "*I don't have to!*" he shouted.

In the face of that indignation, Jyn saw that there was at least some part of him that was right. He hadn't killed her father. And he'd come back to save her rather than let her die there next to him.

She wasn't sure she could handle losing her father and being wrong about Cassian, too. She turned away from him, still reeling from the emotions swirling through her.

Cassian steamed at her for a moment and then turned to K-2SO and began barking orders. "Yavin 4! Make sure they know we're coming in with a stolen ship."

Then he rounded on the rest of them, daring them to take him on. "*Anybody else?*"

No one replied. Not Bodhi, not Chirrut, not Baze.

Not even Jyn.

CHAPTER 33

IN A WAY, Krennic thought, the rebels had done him a favor. He'd already planned to shut down the facility on Eadu, and they'd done an admirable job of that. In fact, they'd gone and killed everyone who could have revealed any of the Death Star's secrets to them.

Of course, the fact that the rebels knew about Eadu in the first place didn't reflect well on Krennic, he knew. Tarkin surely wouldn't see it favorably, and Krennic's worst fears had been confirmed as he was headed back to the Death Star.

That's when he'd received a summons from the Emperor's right hand, Darth Vader himself.

That was never a good thing.

Krennic had met Vader before, and the Sith Lord had rankled him. Krennic considered himself a man of science, and because of that he instantly dismissed Vader's entire religion, based as it was on the so-called Force and other superstitions.

That didn't please Vader, of course, and since Vader had the Emperor's ear, it didn't help Krennic much, either. So at the very least, Krennic always tried to show Vader respect. That wasn't hard, because—ridiculous religion or not—Lord Vader was clearly a dangerous man.

Vader's summons had instructed Krennic to go to his residence on Mustafar, a planet nearly consumed by volcanic activity. Krennic could never understand why Vader would choose to live in such a horrible place—especially given a fact Krennic had discovered while snooping through Imperial Intelligence files for information about the Sith Lord. Mustafar was the planet on which Vader had been so horribly injured decades before.

Those injuries required him to wear that horrible respirator just so he could breathe. It made terrible noises every time what was left of the man inhaled and exhaled. *Hoooo-perrrr. Hoooo-perrrr.*

It sounded like he was just this side of the grave and meant to suck everyone else down with him. When Krennic was in Vader's presence, it took everything he had to ignore it.

When Krennic arrived on Mustafar, he'd ordered his pilot to land next to Vader's monolith, the tall black tower the Sith Lord called home. He'd left his death troopers inside the shuttle and entered the forbidding place alone.

Vader's aide had met him at the door and led him inside to a dim and stifling waiting room that felt something like the inside of an oven. Then Krennic had been forced to wait for Lord Vader like some junior official who had nothing better to do with his time.

This always irritated Krennic, but he didn't see what he could do. Given his precarious position with the Emperor at the moment—mostly due to Tarkin's interference—he couldn't afford to ignore a summons from Vader. It would be seen as a rebuke to the Emperor himself, and that was the absolute last thing Krennic wanted.

So he waited.

Eventually, a door opened on the far end of the meeting chamber, lighting up the darkened room. Krennic heard the man before he saw him. *Hoooo-perrrr. Hoooo-perrrr.*

Then Darth Vader came through that open door, casting his long shadow across the room. Krennic fought what he felt was the natural urge to turn and run.

"Director Krennic," Vader said in a deep and resonant voice, through the ebony mask that concealed all his features. He did not sound pleased.

Krennic reminded himself not to stutter. "Lord Vader."

"You seem unsettled."

Krennic grimaced at that. Of course he was "unsettled." He was practically beside himself with panic. But he couldn't reveal that to Vader.

"No," he said. "Just pressed for time. There's a great many things to attend to."

"My apologies." Vader's tone betrayed no sense of actual regret. "You do have a great many things to explain."

Krennic stiffened his spine. "I've delivered the weapon the Emperor requested. I deserve an audience to make sure he understands its remarkable potential."

He only wanted to make the Emperor see how valuable the Death Star could be—and by extension, how valuable *he* could be. With its power, and the will to use it, they could eliminate war forever and bring eternal peace to the galaxy. The Empire would be made eternal.

But Vader wasn't convinced.

"Its power to create problems has certainly been confirmed. A city destroyed. An Imperial facility openly attacked."

That wasn't Krennic's fault. Everything had been going so well.

"It was Governor Tarkin that suggested the test."

Krennic's attempt to deflect the blame didn't work on Vader.

"You were not summoned here to grovel, Director Krennic."

He was glad to hear that, but if not that, then what? To be executed?

"No, I—"

"There is no Death Star," Vader pronounced. "We're informing the Senate that Jedha was destroyed in a mining disaster."

Krennic knew that claim wouldn't hold up to a close inspection, but the Empire could probably ensure no one ever managed such an investigation. What choice did he have but to agree?

"Yes, my lord."

Vader turned to leave. "I expect you to not rest until you can assure the Emperor that Erso has not compromised this weapon."

It was all Krennic could do not to breathe a loud sigh of relief. "So I'm . . . I'm—I'm still in command."

Vader didn't correct him on that point, and that emboldened Krennic to push further.

"You'll speak to the Emperor about—"

Krennic's voice failed him as an invisible hand seemed to wrap around his throat and begin to cut off his air. He struggled against it, unsure of what to do, since there were no fingers to pry from his neck.

He looked at Vader and saw the man holding a hand toward him, pinching the air, and he knew what was happening. The Sith Lord's faith in his ancient religion suddenly didn't seem so ridiculous anymore.

Krennic wondered if this was it for him. Had Vader only been playing with him before his execution?

"Be careful not to choke on your aspirations, Director."

Then Darth Vader lowered his hand, and as suddenly as it had begun, the pressure on Krennic's throat disappeared. He collapsed to the floor, gasping for air, thankful to still be breathing at all.

CHAPTER 34

AFTER HAVING survived being bombed by rebel forces on Eadu, Jyn couldn't believe she had to put up with listening to the Alliance high council debate whether or not they should give up and let the Empire rule over the galaxy forever.

"We have no recourse but to surrender," said Senator Pamlo of Taris. That set a lot of people talking at once, both for and against the proposal.

Jyn didn't blame people for being scared. She'd seen Jedha be destroyed, after all. She knew exactly how much of a threat the Death Star was.

But to give in immediately, without even a fight? She'd be happy to hold them all responsible for that. Unfortunately, no one was about to give Jyn a vote in the matter.

Senator Bail Organa of Alderaan stood up to protest. "Are we really talking about disbanding something that we've worked so hard to create?"

Admiral Raddus joined in. One of the Mon Calamari, Raddus looked like a grayish fish-man. "We can't just give in," he pleaded.

Senator Vaspar of the Taldot sector begged to disagree. "We joined an alliance, not a suicide pact!"

"We've only now managed to gather our forces," Organa pointed out.

"Gather our forces?" Senator Jebel of Uyter scoffed at the idea that they weren't already at full strength. "General Draven's already blown up an Imperial base!"

General Draven spoke next. As the man in charge of Rebel Intelligence, he was likely responsible for the order to kill Galen Erso, Jyn knew. She understood why he might have done that, although she didn't think she could ever forgive him.

"A decision needed to be made!" said Draven. "By the time we finish talking, there'll be nothing left to defend."

"If it's war you want, you'll fight alone," Pamlo promised.

"If that's the way it's going," Vaspar said, "why have an alliance at all?"

Sharing Draven's impatience, Raddus gestured toward Jyn. "If she's telling the truth, we need to act now!"

Mon Mothma called for order. "Councilors, please!"

The hubbub fell off at that point, but the argument wasn't over.

General Merrick, a pilot with a kind face, leaped into the relative silence. "It is simple. The Empire has the means of mass destruction. The Rebellion does not."

Jebel tried to deny that was even the issue they should be talking about. "The Death Star . . . ? This is nonsense!"

That was all Jyn could take. She might not have a vote on the council, but that didn't mean she didn't have a voice. "What reason would my father have to lie?"

She got up and stood before the others, commanding their attention. "What benefit would it bring him?"

"To lure our forces into a final battle," Draven said. "To destroy us once and for all."

For the head of Rebel Intelligence, it probably paid to be paranoid, but Jyn knew the man was taking it too far.

"Risk everything?" Vaspar said, equally skeptical. "Based on what? The testimony of a criminal. The dying words of her father, an Imperial scientist!"

"But don't forget the Imperial pilot," Jebel countered. Jyn marveled at his ability to argue both sides.

Bodhi stood to one side of the proceedings. He showed absolutely no interest in drawing any attention to himself, much less arguing that the council should take him seriously.

Jyn couldn't believe the distrust being leveled at her. Just because she'd been a criminal didn't mean she'd lie about something so important. "My father gave his life so that we might have a chance to defeat this!"

"So you've told us," said General Dodonna.

"If the Empire has this kind of power, what chance do we have?" Pamlo protested.

Jyn had had enough. "*What chance do we have?* The question is, what choice? Run? Hide? Plead for mercy? *Scatter your forces?*"

Her tone left no room for anyone to dispute how stupid an idea she thought that was. No one interrupted her, so she forged on.

"You give way to an enemy this evil, with this much power, and you condemn the galaxy to an eternity of submission. The time to fight is now! Every moment you waste is another step closer to the ashes of Jedha!"

Someone in the back called out, "What is she proposing?"

Another voice countered, "Just let the girl speak!"

Jyn took that as permission to continue—not that she would have waited for it anyhow. "Send your best troops to Scarif. Send the rebel fleet if you have to. We need to capture the Death Star plans if there is any hope of destroying it."

Pamlo shook her head. "You're asking us to invade an Imperial installation based on nothing but hope."

Jyn gave her a firm nod. "Rebellions are built on hope."

Vaspar disagreed. "There is no hope."

"I say we fight!" said Raddus. Jyn's admiration for the Mon Calamari admiral shot straight up, but would his endorsement be enough?

Not for Jebel, apparently. "And I say the Rebellion is finished!"

Jyn looked to Mon Mothma for help, for some kind of resolution. Instead, she found the formidable woman throwing up her hands. "I'm sorry, Jyn," she said. "Without the full support of the council, the odds are too great."

Jyn stared at her in dismay, then turned to see the rest of the council in agreement with her, no matter how disappointed they might be. Disgusted with them and the entire Rebellion, she turned on her heel and stormed out of the room to let them all rot.

CHAPTER 35

JYN BURST out of the conference room, and Bodhi followed in her wake. They made their way from there into the hangar, where they discovered Chirrut and Baze waiting for them.

"You don't look happy," said Baze.

He had no idea. She'd actually cooled down a bit since she'd left the council chambers.

"They prefer to surrender," Jyn said, glancing back the way they'd come.

"And you?"

"She wants to fight," Chirrut said.

"So do I," Bodhi said. "We all do."

Chirrut pondered this. "The Force is strong."

Jyn looked at the others and actually considered taking them seriously. It would be madness, right? "I'm not sure the four of us is quite enough."

Baze nodded to Bodhi. "How many do we need?"

"What are you talking about?" She'd already counted Bodhi, and the Imperial pilot didn't have any friends in the rebel base, defector or not.

Baze pointed behind her, though, and she turned to see what he meant. More than a dozen soldiers appeared from the hangar's deepest shadows.

They were as rough-looking a group as Jyn had ever seen, and she'd spent time in some of the worst dens of scum and villainy in the galaxy. One was the sergeant who'd led the team that broke her out of prison. He wore the uniform of a special operations soldier, as did most of the rest.

And Cassian stood there in front of them, with K-2SO just behind.

"They were never going to believe you," he said to Jyn.

She fixed him with a cold stare. "I appreciate the support."

"But I do."

She narrowed her eyes at him as she let that sink in.

"I believe you," he said. "We'd like to volunteer. Some of us"—he glanced at the others—"*most* of us, we've all done terrible things on behalf of the Rebellion. Spies. Saboteurs. Assassins."

Jyn scanned the faces lined up to help her. Almost all of them were human, except for K-2SO and a single alien named Pao, a Drabatan from Pipada. Built like a human, he had the face and skin of a dried-out lizard.

No matter where they hailed from, though, they all seemed ready to fight.

"Everything I did, I did for the Rebellion," Cassian explained. "And every time I walked away from something I wanted to forget, I told myself it was for a cause I believed in. A cause that was worth it."

The soldiers behind Cassian nodded in agreement.

"Without that, we're lost. Everything we've done would have been for nothing. I couldn't face myself if I gave up now. None of us could."

Jyn didn't know what to say. She was flattered that Cassian, of all people, would be willing to put his faith in her, much less all the other soldiers. She'd never had so many people willing to put their lives on the line simply because they believed her. Believed *in* her.

But the Alliance high command had considered her demand for action, and they'd already said no. How could they do anything without the Alliance's support? Without its weapons? Its ships?

"It won't be comfortable," Bodhi said to her.

She furrowed her brow at him, confused about what he meant.

"It'll be a bit cramped, but we'll all fit. We could go."

He meant the Imperial cargo shuttle. The one he'd stolen. The one he could just as easily steal again.

Cassian wasn't one to hesitate at any opportunity, even one as slim as this. "Okay," he said to the others, the ones who'd lined up to follow him. "Gear up. Grab anything that's not nailed down."

They hesitated for a moment before they started to move. He waved at them. "Go, go, go!"

Jyn smiled, something she'd doubted she'd get to do that day. She marveled at the soldiers and how quickly they'd decided to stand up and keep fighting, no matter what the odds. Then she realized they'd all been doing that for so long already. It came naturally to them.

K-2SO, who already had everything he needed, spoke to her as the soldiers scattered. "Jyn, I'll be there for you," he said. "Cassian said I had to."

She shook her head at that. Not because the robot had been so brutally honest—she was getting used to that—but at the way Cassian had marshaled support for her.

"I'm not used to people sticking around when things go bad," she told Cassian.

He gave her a casual shrug and a warm smile, as if it was all no big deal. "Welcome home."

Jyn thought that seemed like an odd thing to say, but when she realized she was smiling again, she understood just how perfect Cassian's words were. It had been a long time since she'd felt like she belonged anywhere—or with anyone. Her father's death had hammered that home.

This crew, these people, they were now more her home than any place she'd known since Saw had abandoned her. Despite how insane the mission that had brought them together might be, she discovered she liked it.

CHAPTER 36

JYN AND CASSIAN made their way to the Imperial cargo shuttle, and they found the bay was packed solid. The others were already there—all the people Cassian had brought over before, plus a few more.

That included Chirrut and Baze, who looked like they'd been sitting in the ship the entire time. As Jyn had seen through the viewport, Bodhi had already climbed back in the pilot's seat, and K-2SO had taken the copilot's position once again.

Before she found a seat and sat down, Jyn surveyed the ragtag team of soldiers they'd thrown together—the people with whom she hoped to take down an Imperial installation and save the galaxy. She said the only thing that seemed fitting to her.

"May the Force be with us."

When everyone was settled, Bodhi began rushing through his preflight checklist. As he did, someone in the rebel base's comm center hailed him on the ship's comm.

"Cargo shuttle, we have a pushback request here."

That didn't sound good. No one in the shuttle said a word, trusting Bodhi to handle it. He just kept working to get the starship ready for takeoff.

"Read back, please. Request denied. *You are not cleared for takeoff.*"

Bodhi grimaced and then steeled himself to respond. "Yes,

yes we are. Affirmative." He hesitated for a moment. "Requesting a recheck."

Rather than waiting for a response, Bodhi fired up the shuttle's engines. The rest of the people in the shuttle—Jyn included—belted themselves in. It was either going to be a very short trip or a very fast takeoff.

"I'm not seeing this . . . request here," the person on the other side of the comm said. "What's your call sign?"

Bodhi glanced around, panicked. He had no idea what to say. "Yes, we have it. It's, uh . . . Um . . ."

Bodhi looked to Jyn, but she just shrugged at him. He said the first thing that came into his mind. "Rogue! *Rogue One*."

"There is no 'Rogue One,'" the person on the comm responded.

"There is now," K-2SO said.

Bodhi gunned the engines and took the shuttle into the air.

"Rogue One pulling away," he said.

An instant later, they were gone.

CHAPTER 37

MOST OF the councilors had already left the Rebellion's high council chambers. Some of them had gone to vent their rage about the council's decision. Others were packing up their things to head home and give their people the bad news.

Bail Organa sat there still, unsure of what he should do. What he *could* do. He'd tried his best to sway the council, to get them to see reason, but it had been to no avail.

He'd thought that the news Jyn Erso and Cassian Andor had brought back with them from Jedha would have moved people to courage. Instead, it had set them arguing with each other, divided on whether they could even trust a young woman with such a checkered past.

Never mind that Captain Andor—one of the best agents working for the Rebellion—had vouched for her. Never mind that everything she revealed rang true. There were some who just didn't want to admit she might be right.

Worse, though, were those who believed her story and thought the best thing they could do was surrender. Bail understood the skepticism of some of his fellow councilors when it came to Jyn's story, but he could not stomach the cowardice of the others.

He sat there and stewed about that until Mon Mothma approached him. As the leader of the council, she'd had many things to deal with as the council dispersed, but it seemed she'd concluded her duties. Now they could talk in private— openly and honestly.

"Despite what the others say, war is inevitable," she said.

Bail frowned. What a depressing way to open a conversation. But he had to admit he'd already come to the same conclusion long before.

"I agree," he said. "I must return to Alderaan to inform my people that there will be no peace."

He shook his head. They'd worked so hard to avoid this, to come up with some way to depose the Emperor without devastating what remained of the Republic he'd seized. Now it seemed they'd failed—and badly.

"We will need every advantage," he said.

Mon Mothma recognized what he was saying. If the high council wouldn't agree to support them, they would have to do whatever they could without official backing.

It was more of a risk, of course, but what choice did they have?

Mon Mothma glanced around to make sure no one was listening in. While the chamber had mostly cleared out, it was not entirely empty.

"Your friend," she said in a low voice. "The Jedi."

She was on the same wavelength as him. Obi-Wan Kenobi had been a faithful friend long before he'd become one of the galaxy's most hunted fugitives. Bail didn't want to disturb the man, but things had finally become that desperate.

"He served me well during the Clone Wars and has lived in hiding since the Emperor's purge. Yes, I will send for him."

Would Kenobi answer the call? After so many years living alone—decades, even—would he care enough about the fate of the Republic?

Maybe. If they finally had a chance to stop the Empire? Maybe yes.

"You'll need someone you can trust," Mon Mothma said.

As usual, she was right. Bail couldn't send just anyone to summon Kenobi from his exile. It would have to be someone strong, capable, and utterly committed to the Rebellion.

He could think of only one person. If he could have, he would have chosen anyone else. But it would have to be her.

Bail got to his feet and nodded at Mon Mothma once again. "I would trust her with my life."

CHAPTER 38

BODHI HATED LYING. He just wasn't very good at it.

That was one of the reasons he'd found Saw Gerrera's interrogation of him so laughable. He wouldn't have been able to come up with a good set of lies on the spot if his life had depended on it.

He hadn't needed to lie when he'd abandoned his post and tried to defect to the Rebellion on Jedha. He'd just taken a short leave there. Then he'd gone looking for Saw.

The thought of the destruction of Jedha City still made him ill. All the people he'd ever known growing up—all gone. Murdered by the Empire.

Betraying the Empire had been the right thing to do, but now the only people he could trust were right there in the stolen shuttle with him. And they were depending on him to lie for them.

Otherwise, they'd never land on Scarif, and their mission to find the Death Star's plans would come to a swift and probably fatal end.

As Bodhi flew the shuttle toward Scarif, he rehearsed the lies he'd already made up in his head. He wondered if he should ask Chirrut to pray to the Force for him, but it was too late for that. He wasn't sure if his lies were any good, but they would have to do.

"Okay," he said to the others from the cockpit. "We're coming in. There's a planet-wide defensive shield with a single main entry gate. This shuttle should be equipped with an access code that allows us through."

"Assuming the Empire hasn't logged it as overdue," said K-2SO.

Bodhi wanted to smack the droid, but he knew that would only hurt his hand.

"And if they have?" Jyn asked.

Bodhi shrugged. "Then they shut the gate and we're all annihilated in the cold, dark vacuum of space."

"Not me," said K-2SO. "I can survive in space."

Bodhi was so tempted. . . .

As they neared the gate, Bodhi saw lots of other shuttles and cargo ships moving through it. With luck, they'd get in without any troubles.

There were a couple of Star Destroyers guarding the gate though. That was new. Still, they didn't have much choice. What difference did it make if they were killed by a large ship or a small one?

"Okay, this is good," Bodhi said, trying to rationalize some sense of optimism. "It's not normally this busy. I think this is good."

Maybe the gate controllers wouldn't even notice them. A man could hope, right?

"Okay, here it goes."

He nosed the ship toward the gate. As he went, he turned on the ship's comm so he could speak to the gate controller. "Cargo shuttle SW-0608 requesting a landing pad."

After a short pause, a reply came back. "Cargo shuttle SW-0608, you're not listed on the arrival schedule."

Bodhi could feel everyone in the ship tense up. He tried to

wave off their worries. As an Imperial shuttle pilot, he'd seen mix-ups like that all the time. Honest ones, too.

"Acknowledged, Gate Control. We were rerouted from Eadu flight station. Transmitting clearance code right now."

That wasn't much of a lie. The ship *had* been on Eadu, and they'd rerouted it from there themselves—by stealing it.

Now if only the access code still worked.

K-2SO hit a switch. "Transmitting."

Then they had to wait to learn their fate. Would they be waved through or blown into atoms?

It seemed to take forever. Bodhi glanced back and saw Jyn holding the kyber crystal from her necklace like it was some kind of good-luck charm. Chirrut was too far back for Bodhi to know if he was praying. Either way, though, he'd take all the help he could get.

By the time Gate Control finally spoke up, Bodhi was wondering if he could somehow manage to evade the inevitable attack long enough to make the jump to hyperspace.

"Cargo shuttle SW-0608," the voice finally said. "You are cleared for entry."

Bodhi breathed a silent sigh of relief. They would not be space dust—at least for a little bit longer.

Jyn smiled at him. "I'll tell the others."

Bodhi flew the cargo shuttle through the gate. As he did, he gazed down at the complex below, which sprawled across a cluster of dozens of tropical islands. In other circumstances, Scarif might have been a wonderful place to take a vacation, but the presence of the Empire's data repository there had long since changed all that.

The complex centered on a steely-gray tower called the

Citadel, which spiked out of the main island. There were twenty-five different landing pads on nearby islands arranged in a loose circle around that, and a system of railspeeder lines connected them all to each other.

"SW-0608 clear for landing pad nine," Gate Control said. "Acknowledge please."

Bodhi gave back the standard reply. "SW-0608 proceeding to L-P-nine as instructed." This was all going according to plan so far.

"The main building down there," Cassian said. "What is it?"

"That's the Citadel Tower. If the plans are anywhere, they'll be there."

"And the dish at the top?" Cassian pointed at the Citadel Tower again. "What's it for?"

"That's the communications tower. Every communication in and out of this base goes through that dish."

K-2SO interrupted. "Landing track engaged."

Bodhi got back to the job at hand, preparing the ship for meeting the ground in a peaceable way. "Landing track locked."

"Security?" Cassian said, drawing Bodhi back.

Bodhi shook his head. "I don't know. I've made twenty cargo runs in and out of the place. They've never let me off a landing pad. Security's tight."

As he took the shuttle in for a landing on pad nine, Bodhi wondered if maybe they'd have been better off if the clearance code hadn't worked after all.

CHAPTER 39

JYN GAZED OUT at most of the people who'd decided to join her—including Cassian, Baze, and Chirrut—in their insane attempt to put an end to the Death Star and the Empire's plans for it. There were more than two dozen of them packed into the ship's bay with her—plus Bodhi and K-2SO up in the cockpit—all ready to lay down their lives because they believed in what she'd told the Alliance high command about her father's message.

Scratch that. They were there because they believed in the Rebellion.

"We're landing," Cassian said to her as he rejoined them from the cockpit. "We're coming in!" he added to the rest.

He looked to Jyn, and she realized he wanted her to say something. She'd never been much of a public speaker. She'd never had much that she felt strongly enough about.

Until now.

She looked directly at the rest of them and spoke.

"Saw Gerrera used to say, 'One fighter with a sharp stick and nothing left to lose can take the day.'" She swallowed hard at the thought of the man who had raised her for a time, now gone.

"They have no idea we're coming. They have no reason to expect us. If we can make it to the ground, we'll take the next chance. And the next. On and on until we win or the chances are spent.

"The Death Star plans are down there. Cassian, Kay-Tu, and I will find them. We'll *find* a way to find them."

She looked to Cassian to take over from there. While she might be the spark that lit the fire, she was no commander.

Cassian barked out his orders. "Melshi, Pao, Baze, Chirrut. You'll take the main squad, move east, and get wide of the ship. Find a position between here and the tower.

"Once you get to the best spot, light the place up. Make ten men feel like a hundred. And get those troopers away from us."

"What should I do?" Bodhi asked from the cockpit.

"Keep the engine running," Cassian said. "You're our only way out of here."

Jyn nodded her thanks to Cassian, and he responded in kind. They were about to triumph together or die together. They had to be ready for it either way.

As they landed, Jyn climbed up to the cockpit again to peer out the viewport. She spied four people walking their way: an Imperial officer, two stormtroopers, and a guard.

Over the ship's comm, she heard the guard's voice. "Cargo shuttle SW-0608, be prepared to receive inspection team."

Jyn scrambled back down into the bay and saw that the others had already cleared out into the cargo area underneath the passenger section. She slipped through the hatch and joined them.

"Ready?" she asked.

They all nodded back at her. Baze took the spot closest to the hatch and waited.

She heard the door to the cargo shuttle lower, and the inspection team marched in. Bodhi went down to greet them.

"Hello," the inspection officer said.

"Hey." Bodhi was trying to act casual, but Jyn could hear a tremor in his voice. "You're probably looking for a manifest."

"That would be helpful," the inspection officer said, his voice dripping with sarcasm.

"It's just down here." Bodhi pointed at the hatch.

When they opened the hatch, Baze pointed his rifle up at the inspection team. At the same time, Bodhi pulled his blaster on them, too. Once they saw how many warriors stood there ready to kill them, they surrendered.

The rebels stripped the inspectors and tied them up. While Jyn and Cassian put the stolen uniforms on over their clothes, their prisoners were taken into the cargo bay and stashed there. Meanwhile, Bodhi returned to the ship's controls.

As Jyn emerged in her new outfit, Baze gave her a gentle touch on the arm. "Good luck, little sister."

She could only smile at the hope that gesture gave her in the face of such overwhelming odds.

Up above, Bodhi watched out the window until no one outside was looking at the cargo shuttle. Then he shouted back down into the bay, "Go! Now! You're clear!"

Most of the rebels charged out of the ship. Five of them stayed behind with Bodhi.

Once most of the group was gone, Jyn, Cassian, and K-2SO marched out of the ship in clear daylight. Anyone who spotted them might think they were an Imperial inspection team leaving the cargo shuttle after doing their jobs.

It seemed to be working. So far.

All Jyn could think about was what Baze had said to her. Luck? They were going to need it.

CHAPTER 40

THE BEST thing about Scarif, Orson Krennic thought, was that it wasn't Mustafar. The watery world filled with archipelagos of tropical islands wasn't just entirely unlike a blazing-hot ball of volcanic activity; it also put him well out of the reach of Darth Vader and his horrible Force powers.

Unfortunately, that didn't keep Krennic outside of the Sith Lord's influence. At Vader's insistence, he'd gone to Scarif to make absolutely sure there was no way Galen Erso or anyone else had done anything to compromise the Death Star. To do that, he was going to have to dig deep into Galen's plans.

Krennic would have gone back to Eadu to search through Galen's lab at the research facility, but the rebels had destroyed the entire place. Krennic had to give that to them. They excelled at ruining things.

Just because the facility on Eadu had been turned to rubble didn't mean that Krennic was out of options to pursue, however. Much of Galen's data had been backed up and stored in the vault on Scarif, along with the data of the countless other scientists and engineers who had worked on the project over the years. If Krennic was going to find any troubles with the Death Star, that was the place to look.

That's why he'd gone there in his shuttle, entirely unannounced. The officers walked on eggshells around him, not clear on the nature of his visit, only that he seemed to be in a rage about it. Most of them steered well clear of him, given any kind of chance.

Not everyone had that luxury, however.

Krennic stormed into the Citadel's command center, his death troopers marching behind him. They provided anyone who saw him a clear reminder of not only his rank but his power. He might have to answer to Darth Vader, Grand Moff Tarkin, and even the Emperor himself, but the rest of the Empire had better tremble in fear when he crossed their paths.

General Ramda, the man in charge of the Scarif garrison, personally greeted Krennic when he walked into the room. His confident attitude told Krennic that the man had no idea how much work he was about to put his people through.

"Director," Ramda said. "What brings you to Scarif?"

Krennic dispensed with niceties. He didn't have the time for them most days. Certainly not now.

"Galen Erso. I want every dispatch, every transmission he's ever sent called up for inspection."

Ramda managed not to flinch, but every other officer in the room visibly cringed at the order. It would mean sorting through over a decade's worth of compiled data.

"Every one?"

It was only natural for Ramda to make sure he'd heard Krennic right. Perhaps the question was a quiet plea for mercy. If so, it fell on deaf ears.

"Yes." Krennic spoke in a tone sharp enough to slash through any objections. "*All* of them. Get started."

CHAPTER 41

CASSIAN, JYN, and K-2SO strode up to the railspeeder and boarded it. The guard standing at the train car's doors barely glanced at them. Somewhere out there on the island, the team Baze and Chirrut were leading disappeared into the jungle while the doors closed behind Cassian.

Jyn gave him a nervous look. They had a long way to go, and so many things could trip them up.

K-2SO broke the silence. "I have a bad feeling about—"

"Kay!" Cassian said, scolding the droid. He'd reprogrammed the droid himself, but he'd not been able to work out how to keep him from being so blunt.

Jyn frowned at the machine and softly said, "Quiet."

"What?" K-2SO said, clueless as ever.

The railspeeder carried them directly to the Citadel Tower. It rose in the distance until it loomed over them. As they slowed to a stop in the station, Cassian remarked, "We need a map." Otherwise they'd wind up wandering around lost until someone shot them.

"I'm sure there's one just lying about," K-2SO said. Cassian couldn't always tell if the droid was being sarcastic or not.

"You know what you need to do."

The droid didn't seem to like that, but Cassian wasn't asking. He led the way to another Imperial security droid, which everyone else seemed to be ignoring, standing guard in a corner. As the machine began to say something to them, K-2SO reached out and disabled it, quietly and efficiently.

Sometimes being blunt came in handy, Cassian thought.

Cassian and Jyn turned around, their backs to the altercation between the droids. They blocked the view of anyone who might be curious while K-2SO took down the twin droid and linked himself into a data port in the back of his victim's head. Then he began to drain data from the fallen machine.

When it was over, K-2SO turned around, seeming a little dizzy, as if overwhelmed by everything he'd had to absorb. "Kay?" Cassian asked him, concerned.

The droid shook off the effects of the process. "Our optimal route to the data vault places only eighty-nine stormtroopers in our path. We will make it one third of the way before we are killed."

That wasn't going to work. They were going to need help.

Cassian pulled out his comm and spoke into it quietly. "Melshi. Talk to me."

A long moment later, the rebel sergeant replied. "Ready, ready. Standing by."

Cassian turned to Jyn for confirmation, to make sure she was ready. She gave him a firm nod.

"Light it up," Cassian said into the comm.

Since the moment they'd disappeared into the jungle, Melshi's team had been sticking explosives all over the complex. At Cassian's signal, Melshi detonated them.

The rebels had been busy. The blasts went off in every direction. Alarms sounded soon after, and everyone in the tower went on alert.

A massive patrol of stormtroopers came charging down the hallway, heading straight for Cassian, Jyn, and K-2SO. They all had their rifles out and ready, and Cassian couldn't help holding his breath as they rushed toward him.

A moment later, though, they rewarded his patience by marching straight past. They were headed for the atrium behind Cassian, from which they could head to the beach and challenge any attackers.

Cassian and Jyn didn't have to wait long before the rebels opened fire on the stormtroopers, picking them off one by one.

CHAPTER 42

MANY LIGHT-YEARS AWAY, Grand Moff Tarkin stared out a viewport on the Death Star. While Orson Krennic may have felt that he was the man who'd brought the Death Star to life, it was Tarkin who'd conjured the vision of the battle station in the first place. Not only would he take credit for the project in the Emperor's mind—he would be the one to employ it.

Tarkin had made sure of that from the start. Krennic was a fine person to get the Death Star up and running, his lack of consideration for security aside. But the Emperor would never put such a powerful weapon in the hands of a man with such limited ambitions.

Krennic only wanted to *build* an amazing weapon. He had no real desire to *use* it.

But what good was power if you didn't wield it?

The only real question was, What should Tarkin use the Death Star against? What would make for the best display of its awesome power?

General Romodi walked in, disturbing his train of thought.

"Sir?" Romodi said. "Scarif base! They're reporting a rebel incursion."

That seemed odd. Scarif was well protected. Why would the rebels risk destruction by attacking it?

"I want to speak with Director Krennic." While the man might not have had enough hunger for power, his insight on this matter might prove useful.

"He's *there*, sir. On Scarif."

Tarkin arched his eyebrows as he considered this news. Something had put both the rebels and Krennic on Scarif. That could not be a coincidence.

"The original plans for this station are kept there, are they not?" he asked.

"They are."

Tarkin frowned. It seemed clear now that Krennic had been far more careless about the security of the battle station than Tarkin had suspected. He would be forced to cauterize the problem and put a swift end to it.

He nodded at Romodi. "Prepare for the jump to hyperspace, and inform Lord Vader."

Tarkin was confident he could handle the situation himself, with the power of the Death Star at hand. However, having Vader around to bear witness to his newfound might could impress upon the Sith Lord who was truly in charge.

As Romodi rushed off, Tarkin allowed a hint of a smile to play across his lips. Perhaps this wouldn't come out so bad for him after all.

CHAPTER 43

A COMM PRIVATE raced through the crowded hangar in the rebel headquarters on Yavin 4. He'd just gotten the most amazing news, and he had to get it to the high council—or at least what was left of it on the green moon—as soon as possible. He spotted Mon Mothma standing at one side of the central command area, and he shouted for her.

"Senator! Senator!"

Mon Mothma cringed a little inside, as she was no longer officially a senator. The Emperor had stripped her of that role after she'd publicly condemned him, and she'd been forced to flee into exile. Still, her fellow citizens—not the Emperor—had elected her to that position, so in her mind the title remained hers.

She turned at the sound of the comm private's voice and made to speak with the man. Before he could reach her, though, General Draven and General Merrick stepped in front of him, cutting him off. Merrick actually grabbed the man by his uniform and shouted into his face.

"Stop right there, Private!" the general thundered.

Mon Mothma wasn't about to let Merrick get between her and whatever news the private had. She rushed toward him, shouting, "Let him speak!"

The private ignored the general's scowl. He'd been told to report to Mon Mothma, and he wasn't going to let anyone stop him, generals or not.

"Intercepted Imperial transmission, ma'am," he said. "Rebels on Scarif."

Mon Mothma's jaw dropped in surprise, but she covered for it quickly. Who would have thought that this moment would come so soon? She'd hoped for it, of course, but she'd thought she might not find out about it until Cassian and Jyn had returned triumphant—or she'd heard reports of their deaths.

"I need to speak with Admiral Raddus," she said to the private. The Mon Calamari warmaster would know what to do about this.

How could they respond? How many ships did they have ready? How fast could they get there?

Most important of all, was it worth the risk?

The private shook his head. "He's returned to his ship. He's gone to fight!"

Draven and Merrick glanced at Mon Mothma then, and she had to do her best to suppress a smile. She was pleased that Jyn and Cassian had gone to Scarif to complete the mission the high command didn't have the stomach to back. Now Raddus might also make sure they got the help they deserved.

The two generals scrambled off to see what they could do about it, but Mothma knew they were already too late. There would still be ships hurrying to catch up with Raddus in orbit, but none of them would refuse the admiral's orders to join him in jumping to Scarif.

As Mon Mothma strolled through the hangar and watched the various ships prepare to leave, she spotted a pair of droids rushing through. She'd seen them with Bail Organa in the past, but she believed they were with Captain Raymus Antilles now.

The golden protocol droid—C-3PO, she thought—chased after a blue-and-silver astromech, calling after him as he went.

"Scarif?" the droid said. "They're going to Scarif? Why does nobody ever tell me anything, Artoo?"

Sometimes Mon Mothma wanted to ask the exact same thing. Right now, though, she felt grateful that someone had found the guts to do what needed to be done, without letting her know anything about it.

CHAPTER 44

BODHI HATED explosions. As a cargo pilot, he knew that when things started blowing up, everything had gone wrong.

Still, he felt pleased to hear the bombs Melshi and the others had set. They didn't even need to hurt anyone, although Bodhi didn't think the rebels would mind if they did. The explosions just needed to grab Imperial attention and keep it focused outside of the Citadel for as long as possible. That was the kind of chaos Cassian and Jyn needed if they were going to get into the Citadel, much less all the way down to the data vault.

Bodhi watched through the cargo shuttle's viewport and saw blaster fire lighting up the air. One of the rebels had brought along a rocket launcher, too, and they'd fired it into the stormtroopers, wreaking even more chaos.

An officer in the Citadel's central command screamed out orders over their comm system, and people on the pads—either officers or stormtroopers—answered. She couldn't make sense of all of it, but enough of it came through loud and clear.

"Pad Twelve! Close it down!"

"Taking fire!"

"Coming on your flank!"

"Pad Twelve!"

"Pad Fourteen requesting assistance!"

"I need numbers!"

"Unknown! Unknown!"

"Pad Fourteen, what's going on down there? Status, please!"

"We have rebels everywhere!"

"All pads report in immediately!"

To Bodhi, that sounded like an invitation to help sow chaos. He activated his ship's radio and started shouting into it. "Pad Two! This is Pad Two! We count forty rebel soldiers running west off pad two!"

Of course, Bodhi was actually on pad nine, and there was nothing of the sort happening on pad two. He'd watched the rebels run into the jungle, and he'd done his best to track them from there. They might have set off an explosion at pad two, but none of them was still there. If the stormtroopers raced over there to help out, they'd find no rebels to attack.

Anything he could do to waste the Empire's time.

Bodhi handed the ship's microphone to Corporal Tonc, one of the rebels who'd stayed behind in the cargo shuttle.

"Tell them you're pinned down by rebels on pad five."

Tonc smiled at the order and set straight to it. "This is Pad Five! We're being overrun!"

The commander in the Citadel responded as best he could. "Pad Twelve! Pad Ten! Pad Eight! Please confirm! Confirm and report! Get reinforcements down to pad five immediately!"

Bodhi had to smile at that. To think, they could destroy the Empire's response to their attack with just a few well-placed words.

He worried, though, about what would happen when the Empire turned its blasters toward him.

CHAPTER 45

CHIRRUT HAD not ever expected to find himself on another planet, fighting to help destroy the deadliest weapon in the galaxy. But after the Death Star blew his hometown—Jedha City—to pieces, he didn't have anything else to do or anywhere else to go.

He'd lost almost everything in that attack: his friends, his family—even the Holy City itself. The only thing he had left was his faith in the Force and his best friend, Baze.

That was what had taken him to Scarif. It would have been easy for him to plead off after Cassian and Jyn had taken him to Yavin 4. He was blind, after all, and most people expected less of him because of that. He could have asked to be led away from all this, and no one would have questioned his choice.

He would have known, though, and so would Baze. Just because he couldn't see didn't mean he couldn't be useful in the fight against the Empire. And if there was any chance at all that he could help stop the Empire from using the Death Star to utterly conquer the entire galaxy, how could he walk away from that?

He had the echo-box transmitter on his belt; that helped him figure out where he was in the world. Plus he had Baze. And most important, he still had his faith in the Force.

So he'd gone with Baze and the rebel commandos and helped them place their bombs on the various landing pads situated around the Citadel. Then, after Sergeant Melshi had detonated them, Chirrut had also joined the fight.

For a while, it seemed like the rebels had the upper hand. They had hidden themselves well, and the stormtroopers were having a hard time finding them. The stormtroopers also had only blaster rifles to defend themselves with, and the rebels could pick them off from cover without much fear.

But then Chirrut heard something he'd never heard before. It thrummed like a herd of engines, but it also lurched forward with a gigantic gait, like that of a beast several stories tall. The others couldn't see what it was through all the smoke the bombs had thrown up, but such things didn't distract Chirrut. They couldn't.

He heard them coming, whatever they were, and he knew what he had to do. "Baze!" he shouted. *"Baze!"*

He heard his old friend hesitate. Baze stopped firing his weapon for a moment, the souped-up blaster with the ammo tank he carried on his back. He froze there and said, "What?"

While Baze listened for what Chirrut had already heard, Chirrut turned and bolted away from the things coming toward them. As he did, he shouted, "Run. Run!"

The gigantic walking machines emerged from the smoke then, like ancient monsters shambling forth from their lairs. Chirrut heard someone call them by name: AT-ACTs.

Whatever they were called, the massive machines opened fire on the rebels. Blaster fire erupted all around Chirrut as he raced for cover with Baze right behind him. Explosions seemed to surround them, but they weren't about to give up.

Chirrut knew the real battle was just starting.

CHAPTER 46

WITH ALL the chaos going on outside the Citadel, it wasn't hard for Jyn, Cassian, and K-2SO to find their way to the data vault. All the stormtroopers had been ordered outside to deal with the rebel assault, leaving only a skeleton crew of officers to staff the place.

When they reached the data vault, only a single officer stood between them and their target. He looked up at them curiously, surprised to find people trying to access the data vault when they probably should have been trying to help repel the attack.

"Can I help you?" he said.

"That won't be necessary," K-2SO said.

The droid stepped forward and clocked the officer on top of the head with a steely hand. The man collapsed without another word.

K-2SO set to work at the console where the Imperial officer had been standing. According to what he had downloaded from the local security droid, getting into the data vault required at least two people. One person had to work the console while someone else walked into the actual data vault.

He sent Cassian and Jyn ahead of him while he took control of the console. "Take him with you," he said. "You'll need his handprint to open the inner door to the vault."

Cassian and Jyn grabbed the officer, each taking him under an armpit, and dragged him through the outer door to the vault, which stood open. At the other end of a short tube,

146

they came to the hand scanner K-2SO had described to them, and they put the officer's palm on it.

The door didn't budge.

"It's not working!" Cassian shouted.

K-2SO knew what the problem was without even looking. *"Right* hand."

Cassian grabbed the officer's other hand and slapped it on the scanner. A moment later, the inner vault door opened.

CHAPTER 47

THE REBEL FLEET—such as it was—slipped out of hyperspace high above Scarif. The first wave included starships of all kinds and sizes: X-wings, Y-wings, U-wings, and even Admiral Raddus's cruiser, the *Profundity*. More slipped in behind them every moment.

General Merrick liked to lead from the front, entering the battle in his own X-wing. The rebel fleet was far too small for someone of his skills to sit in a capital ship, sheltered from the heart of the fight. He had to be right in the mix.

"This is Blue Leader," he said as he got his bearings. Hyperspace always made him a little disoriented. "All squadron leaders report in."

Gold Leader, Red Leader, and Green Leader all squawked back at him, confirming they'd made it to their proper destination. Merrick allowed himself a thin smile of relief. So far, at least, the plan had gone flawlessly. Of course, the shooting hadn't started yet.

The rest of the plan involved getting inside the shield around Scarif before the Empire had the chance to seal the planet off from them. Otherwise, getting through the shield would be next to impossible, especially with a pair of Imperial Star Destroyers standing guard over it. They had to move fast.

A familiar gravelly voice came over the comm. "This is Admiral Raddus. Red and Gold Squadrons, engage those two Star Destroyers. Blue Squadron, get to the surface before they close that gate!"

"Copy you, Admiral." Just as they'd discussed. Merrick was already heading toward the gate. "Blue Squadron, on me!" he barked.

One by one, the members of Blue Squadron checked in, confirming they were ready and understood their orders. "Copy, Blue Leader!"

Even as they raced for the gate, though, Merrick could see the Imperials had spotted them. The edges of the gate had already started to come together, and they would have to hustle if they wanted to make it through.

Blue Four and Six had lagged behind a bit, but they were determined to slip through the closing gate. "Come on, come on, come on, *come on!*" Blue Six said, shouting at their engines as they barreled toward the planet and the nearly invisible shield.

Blue Four could see, though, that they weren't going to make it. He hauled back on his stick to peel away from the shield just in time, and he shouted for Blue Six to do the same. *"Pull up!"*

Merrick didn't know if Blue Six had kept his X-wing at top speed the entire time or not. Would another second of acceleration have made a difference? They would never know.

Blue Six smashed into the shield, which had fully closed. The X-wing exploded in a bright ball of fire.

The rest of Blue Squadron had gotten through. They were trapped inside the shield, along with the rebel commandos who were already on the ground—the people they'd gone to help in their desperate attempt to grab the Death Star's plans.

General Merrick gritted his teeth and set to leading his squadron in doing its job. Blue Squadron had made its choice about where it would stand that day, and it was time to face its doom.

CHAPTER 48

JYN AND CASSIAN hauled the unconscious Imperial officer back out of the tube that led to the data vault. With the inner door open, thanks to the use of his hand, he would only be in the way.

As they deposited the man on the floor, K-2SO looked up at them. He was plugged into the console and was supposed to be monitoring Imperial communications to see if anyone was coming their way. When he started to speak, Jyn expected nothing but bad news from him.

Instead he said, "The rebel fleet has arrived."

That stunned Jyn and Cassian both. "What?" she said, confused.

When they'd left Yavin 4, she'd been sure no one else would come after them—unless it might be to arrest them. If the rebel fleet had shown up, though, it hadn't come just to offer moral support. It was joining the fight!

But K-2SO had more to tell them, and little of it was good. "There's fighting on the beach. They've locked down the base. They've closed the shield gate."

If Jyn's heart had soared a moment before, it now came crashing down. "What does that mean?" She looked to Cassian. "We're trapped?"

He nodded at her.

"We have to tell them we're down here!" she said to K-2SO. "We're close!"

"We haven't much time," K-2SO said. "We could transmit

the plans to the rebel fleet. We'd have to get a signal out to tell them it's coming. It's the size of the data files. That's the problem. They'll never get through. Someone has to take that shield gate down."

Cassian pulled out his comm and began talking into it. "Bodhi! Bodhi, can you hear me?"

No answer.

"Tell me you're out there! Bodhi!"

The cargo pilot's voice came back. He sounded a little shaken. "I'm here. We're standing by. They've started fighting. The base is on lockdown!"

"I know," Cassian said. "*Listen to me*. The rebel fleet is up there. You've got to tell them they've gotta blow a hole in the shield gate so we can transmit the plans—"

"I can't," Bodhi complained. "I'm not tied into the comm tower. We're not tied in—"

Cassian didn't want to hear it. "Find a way!" Then he turned to K-2SO. "Cover our backs."

As Cassian headed for the tube, Jyn hesitated.

She took the blaster from the unconscious Imperial officer and offered it to K-2SO. "You'll need this," she said.

The droid just looked at it for a moment, unsure of what to do. She held the blaster up in front of him. "You wanted one, right?"

K-2SO reached out and took the blaster. He stared at it in his hands. "Your behavior, Jyn Erso, is continually unexpected."

That brought a smile to her face.

Cassian had already made it into the tube that led into the vault. He turned back and called for her. "Jyn, come on."

She turned to follow him, hoping she wouldn't regret what she'd just done.

CHAPTER 49

BODHI STARED at the comm system for a moment, unsure what to do. Outside, he saw AT-ACTs heading for the rebel commandos, and he froze. What could he do to prevent those walking tanks from killing them all?

Baze stood up then, and he had a rocket launcher hoisted over his shoulder. He aimed it at the nearest AT-ACT and pulled the trigger. A rocket blasted out of the launcher and smashed right into the front of the machine, catching it on the side of the cockpit like a boxer's right cross.

For a moment, Bodhi thought that might do the trick and bring the walker down. The gigantic machine just shook off the attack, though, and kept going.

Baze, Chirrut, and anyone else standing near them was doomed, Bodhi knew. They couldn't outrun a machine like that, and they had no way to stop it.

Another missile streamed out of the sky just then and exploded against the side of the AT-ACT. The blast shook the machine, and smoke began pouring from it.

Bodhi scanned the sky to see where the help had come from, and he spotted a fleet of X-wings zooming overhead. The rebels on the beach sent up a cheer, and Bodhi joined them.

Hope surging in him, Bodhi slid down from the cockpit and into the shuttle's cabin. Corporal Tonc was right behind him.

"All right," he said to the others. "Listen up. We're going to have to go out there."

They stared at him. It was literally a war zone outside, and no one wanted to leave the relative safety of the cargo shuttle. Bodhi didn't wait for them though. He began gathering up the gear he needed.

"What're you doing?" Tonc asked.

"They closed the shield gate," Bodhi said. "We're stuck here. But the rebel fleet are pulling in. We just have to get a signal strong enough to get through to them and let them know we're trapped down here.

"For that we need to connect to the communications tower. Now, I can patch us in over here, the landing pad, but *you* have to get on the radio. Get one of the guys out there to find a master switch. Get them to activate the connection between us and that comms tower, okay?"

Tonc glanced at the others. He seemed to be the one selected for the job by default.

"Then go!" Bodhi shouted at him.

Tonc went.

CHAPTER 50

JYN FOLLOWED Cassian through the tube and into the data vault proper. It was a circular tower—towers, really—of tapes sealed off behind a large panel of glass. The towers seemed to stretch to a dizzying height and depth from where they stood. They contained a boggling amount of information gathered from all across the Empire.

Jyn's heart leaped into her throat. How would they locate the tape they wanted?

K-2SO spoke to them over the vault's intercom system. "Schematics bank. Data tower two."

Cassian gaped up at the tower in question. *"How do I find that?"*

"Searching . . ."

A moment later, K-2SO spoke up again. "I can locate the tape, but you'll need the handles for extraction."

Jyn gestured to a set of controls that worked a pair of mechanical arms on the other side of the glass. Cassian dashed over and grabbed them, but he couldn't seem to make sense of them. "What are we supposed to do with this?"

Behind the glass, Jyn spotted a retrieval arm whipping through the columns above them. Without notice, the arm stopped cold. Then, in a flash, it zipped closer and came to a halt again, hovering in place. The controls, Jyn saw, could work the arm to grab a tape and bring it to them. All they had to do—still—was find the right tape.

Jyn heard someone rushing into the room where K-2SO

was, and she was relieved that she'd given the droid that spare blaster. He was likely going to need it.

The door at the end of the tube closed on its own. K-2SO must have done it, she hoped, to protect them.

Over the intercom, she heard the droid talking to someone.

"The rebels. They went . . . over there!"

Confused, Cassian called out. "Kay-Tu! What's going on out there?"

"There's one," the droid said, clearly talking to whoever had interrupted him out there.

Then there was a huge commotion. Jyn heard K-2SO's servos moving about, mixed in with voices grunting in pain. Then a blaster shot rang out, but without a cry of pain following it. A moment later another shot sang, and this time Jyn heard what sounded like an armored figure collapsing. A stormtrooper, she guessed.

The fight was over, but was K-2SO all right? And if not, could they find the tape without him?

CHAPTER 51

SERGEANT MELSHI looked up at the sky to see the rebel ships dogfighting with their Imperial foes overhead. He felt grateful for the assistance, but he knew that such a fight meant the Empire would have closed the shield around the planet. He hoped the larger rebel ships that had brought the fighters could manage to punch a hole through that shield soon, or he and his troops would be stuck on Scarif for the entirety of their terribly shortened lives.

Meanwhile, Melshi had more pressing matters demanding his attention on the planet's surface. Blue Squadron had been a huge help with the AT-ACTs, but there were TIE strikers, with their sharp, streamlined wings, inside the shield, too, harassing the rebel pilots every step of the way.

Through the raucous noise of the battle, Melshi heard Corporal Tonc trying to raise him over the comms. "Melshi! Listen up! Bodhi will send the signal from here—he's patching us in—but you guys have to open up the line to the tower."

Melshi understood at least part of that. Bodhi wanted to get a message to the rebel fleet but couldn't get the signal through the shield on his own. They needed to help him. "How?" Melshi said. "Please advise."

"There's a master switch at every hub," Tonc said. "Find the hub!"

Melshi scanned the nearest hub, which wasn't all that far away, but he didn't see what Tonc was talking about. He was a soldier, not a communication tech. "Master switch? *Describe*. What are we looking for?"

Melshi heard Tonc yell at someone else inside the cargo shuttle. "What does it look like?" he said. "The master switch! Where is it?"

Tonc relayed the description back from the Imperial defector, Bodhi. Melshi frowned at every word. It would be hard enough to get to a landing pad, much less to find a switch and activate it.

He hoped the effort would be worth it. From the way the battle raging above them seemed to be going, they didn't have much time left.

CHAPTER 52

FINDING THE TAPE was proving to be a real challenge. Cassian worked the controls of the data retrieval system while Jyn read labels of various tapes off the console in front of her.

"'Hyperspace tracking' . . . 'Navigational systems' . . ." None of them seemed to have anything to do with the flaw in the Death Star that her father had told her about.

K-2SO tried coaching them through it from his side of the intercom system. "Two screens down," he said.

Jyn did as the droid asked, bringing up yet another list of labels that meant little to nothing to her. K-2SO scanned them faster than she could, though, and he spotted something worth yelling about.

"'Structural engineering'!" he shouted. "Open that!"

Jyn did as requested, and she heard the sound of the blaster she'd given to K-2SO firing again. More stormtroopers must have been trying to take him out. No matter how good the droid might be with the weapon, they'd overwhelm him with numbers soon enough, and then they'd come for Cassian and her.

Jyn scrolled through the files, reading off the labels as she went. "'Project code names' . . . 'Stellar Sphere' . . . 'Mark Omega' . . . 'Pax Aurora' . . ."

None of it made any sense to her. They'd gone from being descriptions to code names, and she had no context by which she could interpret them.

"'War-Mantle' . . . 'Cluster Prism' . . . 'Black Saber' . . ."

Then she spotted exactly what she was looking for, whether she'd known it or not.

"'Stardust,'" she said. "It's that one."

"How do you know that?" Cassian asked. He'd been just as mystified as her until that moment.

It was the name her father had always called her. "I know because it's me."

CHAPTER 53

BODHI DIDN'T like this one bit. He'd told Tonc what the master switch looked like, and the private had relayed the description to his sergeant. Now, though, Bodhi needed to make the connection on his end. He had to walk out on the landing pad and use a cable to attach the cargo shuttle to the Citadel's communications system. Otherwise, the work that Melshi and the others were risking their lives to do would be for nothing.

That meant leaving the safety of the ship. That was something Bodhi had known might happen but had been hoping against ever since they'd set down on Scarif.

He wished he could just send some of the rebel commandos out to do the job while he sat safe in the cargo shuttle and pretended he was still a loyal Imperial pilot. They didn't know how to hook up the communications cable though. He could do it faster than any of them, which meant there was less chance of his being shot.

At a nod from Bodhi, the rest of the commandos still in the ship moved into the open air and spread themselves out around the landing pad. They offered him protection from incoming fire while he did his job, but Bodhi wondered if they might attract just as much trouble instead.

It was too late to question it any longer. Bodhi charged out of the cargo shuttle, toting a spooled cable pack on his back.

He reached the place where he needed to make the connection, without anyone shooting at him. Breathing a grateful sigh, he pulled the end of the cable out of the pack and plugged it into the comm station. Then he spun around and ran back the way he had come.

He had almost reached the shuttle when the cable snagged on something. He had to go back to untangle it.

He found the kink in the cable fast enough, but that didn't do him much good. As he knelt there and tried to untangle it, a car arrived on the railspeeder and a patrol of stormtroopers spilled out of it. They spotted him instantly and marched straight toward him.

"Hey, you!" the one in the lead said. "Identify yourself."

Bodhi stood up slowly. Maybe he could talk his way out of this. Maybe word that he'd defected hadn't reached Scarif yet.

"I can explai—"

A blaster shot from one of the rebel commandos cut him off, and Bodhi found himself in the middle of an instant battle. Bolts flew past him from every direction, and he wondered not only how long he had to live but which side would wind up shooting him in the end.

CHAPTER 54

K-2SO KNEW he was in trouble. He'd already been shot in the back once, and it was only a matter of time before the other stormtroopers assaulting the data vault took him down.

He was grateful that Jyn had given him a blaster. Without it, the stormtroopers would have overwhelmed him long before. Their reluctance to believe that an Imperial security droid could possibly have been reprogrammed to work against them had helped him at first, but they had spread the word that there was a rogue droid in the entrance to the data vault. They showed no hesitation about trying to destroy him now.

Despite the fact he was dealing with armed foes actively trying to kill him, K-2SO still needed to help Cassian, the man who'd personally reprogrammed him in the first place. Cassian shouted for him over the intercom again. "Kay! We need the file for Stardust!"

The blasts from the stormtroopers' rifles fell on the droid like sideways rain, and he moved like he could dance between the drops. A few blasts glanced off him here and there, but for the most part, he managed to avoid them.

It would have been so easy to just lie down on the ground and pretend he had malfunctioned, but K-2SO wasn't programmed that way. While Cassian sometimes complained about how blunt the droid was when he spoke, that was rooted directly in how honest Cassian had made him.

Cassian had also made him selfless. Not only did he not think of people's feelings, he didn't think of his own needs much, either. If Cassian needed something so he could save the entire galaxy, then K-2SO was bound to find a way to give it to him, no matter what the odds of survival might be.

K-2SO reached for the console and ordered up the tape labeled *Stardust*. The retrieval arm would locate it soon.

The droid heard Jyn coaching Cassian in the use of the retrieval arm. "That's it! You almost have it!"

In just a moment, they should have the prize they'd come for. From there, K-2SO could try to figure out if there was any escape from the Citadel, no matter how dire his calculations concerning that might seem.

Before that happened, though, a blast struck the console in front of the droid and blew it up. The explosion knocked him backward and loosed every circuit in his body. As he staggered forward, he noticed that parts of him had been knocked not just loose but free. They dangled from his battered frame by the thinnest of wires.

"Climb!" he shouted at the intercom.

He had to protect the console. If the stormtroopers reached it, they could use it to open the door to the data vault, and soon after that they would either capture or—more likely—kill Cassian and Jyn.

"Climb the tower! Send the plans to the fleet! If they open the shield gate, you can broadcast from the tower!"

It was then that K-2SO realized he didn't need to protect the console any longer. In fact, he could no longer manage it. The best thing to do, then, was to destroy it. That way, the door would never open.

At least not until after Cassian and Jyn had grabbed the tape and gotten away.

"Kay!" Cassian yelled.

The droid could hear the anguish in the man's voice. They'd put a lot of work into each other, after all. But without K-2SO performing this final act, Cassian and Jyn had almost zero chance of completing their mission. Even with his help, they'd face nearly impossible odds.

Nearly.

He fell on the display and tore into it as the blasts smashed into his body. He kept at it until his limbs had been blown away, until his motors stopped working, until all his circuits were dead.

As K-2SO's mind faded to black, one last thought passed through it.

That door would never open again.

CHAPTER 55

KRENNIC HAD THOUGHT he'd already had the worst week of his life. Worse even than the one during which Galen Erso had abandoned their work on the Death Star and gone into hiding, leaving Krennic alone to head up the project.

He'd already lost control of the Death Star to Grand Moff Tarkin. He'd been threatened by Darth Vader. And he suspected if he failed at his current task, he would probably be executed, perhaps by the Emperor's own hand.

But this week kept finding ways to become even worse.

The rebel fleet should have fled as soon as it saw how outmatched it was. Instead, it had fought like a cornered rancor, desperate to tear apart anything nearby. The rebels couldn't possibly prevail against the two Star Destroyers in orbit over the planet—not to mention the TIE fighters and TIE strikers swarming about the place—but they could certainly bloody the Empire's nose before they went down.

Was that really their only goal? To make a final, pointless gesture of defiance before the ascendancy of the Death Star rendered the Rebel Alliance moot?

The rebels had focused most of their firepower at the Star Destroyers, but they'd also made a strong effort against the gate. Krennic didn't see how they could hope to penetrate the shield. It had been built to last.

Still, they refused to stop trying. They'd even sent a squadron of Y-wings to make a bombing run. As if they could simply batter down the gate like a wooden door on an ancient castle.

It wasn't like they would be able to break a hole in the shield large enough for any of the rebel ships on Scarif to escape through it. The rebels trapped inside would be rooted out and destroyed, one by one, like the vermin they were.

But the Y-wings had done more than slap the Star Destroyers around. They'd actually managed to disable the electronics on one of the gigantic starships with an ion bomb. It wasn't a permanent condition, but until the crews on the Star Destroyer managed to fix it, the craft was floating dead in space, a sitting womp rat for the rebels' weaponry.

And then Krennic got word that his worst suspicions were true. Lieutenant Adema relayed a report to him and said, "Unauthorized access at the data vault."

"What?"

Krennic froze, unable to believe the news for a moment, but then it all made sense. The attack on the ground. The appearance of the rebel fleet. They were all there for one thing. The last thing Krennic wanted them to find.

The Death Star's plans.

"It's just come in, sir."

At least now Krennic knew what was at stake, and he knew what he had to do.

"Send my guard squadron to the battle!" The death troopers would help break the back of the rebel assault, but Krennic had to hit the heart of the problem himself. "Two men with me! Get that beach under control!"

Krennic shoved his way out of the room, leaving others to worry about the rest of the battle. If he wanted whatever was going on in the data vault stopped, he would have to put an end to it himself.

CHAPTER 56

BODHI HAD never been so scared in his life. Not when Galen Erso had approached him about betraying the Empire. Not when he'd finally defected to join the rebels. Not even when Bor Gullet had probed his mind.

The battle on landing pad nine raged about him. Blaster fire whizzed so close he could feel its heat on his skin.

Corporal Tonc tried to be brave. He stood up and started firing back at the stormtroopers. For his courage, he was shot dead.

Bodhi gawked at the young man in horror. Just a moment before, he'd been fighting against the Empire, and then he was gone. The only thing Bodhi could do was hunker down with his still unconnected communications cable and hope it all ended before he took a fatal blast, too.

Then Cassian started shouting at him again through the comm.

"Bodhi, are you there?"

The pilot's heart leaped with hope. Cassian had saved him before. Maybe he could do it again.

"I'm here. I'm here! I'm pinned down! I can't get to the ship."

He stared at the Imperial cargo shuttle he'd stolen on Eadu. It wasn't actually all that far away. A quick dash, and he'd be inside it for sure.

But blaster bolts filled the air between it and him. The same kind that had cut down Tonc, a trained soldier.

"I can't plug in!" Bodhi said, trying to explain.

"You have to!" said Cassian. "They have to hit that gate! If the shield's open, we can send the plans!"

Bodhi cringed. Cassian wasn't coming to save him. The man was going to get him killed instead.

Still, Bodhi knew Cassian was right. If he didn't get that cable plugged in, it would all be for nothing. Tonc's death. The rest of the commandos'.

Even—when the stormtroopers finally caught up with him—his own end.

It would all be in vain.

Bodhi couldn't let that happen, not without giving that cable his best shot. He gritted his teeth and braced himself.

He charged across the open space between his hiding place and the shuttle. Blaster fire singed him from all sides, but not one of the shots struck true. He made it back to the shuttle and slammed the unattached end of the cable home.

Bodhi didn't have time to collapse in relief. He snatched up the ship's radio and turned it on.

"Melshi! Melshi! Come in, please! Anybody out there?"

No one answered.

"Rogue One! Rogue One! Anybody?"

CHAPTER 57

WITH THE CONSOLE K-2SO had been protecting now destroyed, Jyn and Cassian had no way to get the tape labeled *Stardust*. At least not with the retrieval arm Cassian had been controlling. Without the console's power, it had frozen in place.

Jyn stared up at the glass separating them from the data tower, and she realized something. If the system couldn't bring the tape to them, they'd have to go get it themselves.

She drew the Imperial blaster from the stolen holster on her hip. "Step back," she said to Cassian.

As he cleared the way, she pointed the blaster at the glass and fired. The window shattered. Now there was nothing between them and their goal.

Nothing but a steep and dangerous climb up a data tower that had never been meant to be accessed that way.

Jyn's stolen uniform would be too restrictive for such a task. It was meant for ordering people around, not scrambling up precarious towers. She slipped it off of her regular clothes, which she'd kept on underneath, and Cassian did the same.

Once free of the Imperial outfit, Jyn went through the broken window and leaped for the data tower. It wasn't so far away, but the drop below it was long—probably fatal.

She made it and began climbing to where she knew the Stardust tape sat, roughly two or three stories above her. She could see the retrieval arm stuck there, right where it had reached out to grab the tape.

Cassian followed right behind, only not as fast. Jyn was lighter and more nimble, and she moved faster than he did. Perhaps life on the run had better prepared her for such challenges.

The inside of the data tower roared with noise. Far above, some kind of ventilation system pumped air in and out of the tower at a nearly deafening volume, keeping the tapes cool.

Jyn raced for the Stardust tape, determined to grab it as soon as she could—and not to let it fall. She reached out and plucked it right from the frozen retrieval arm's grip.

"I've got it!" she shouted.

She glanced back down at Cassian and nearly lost her grip.

"Careful!" he said, still far below her. "You okay?"

She didn't stop to respond. She just tucked the tape into a pocket in her vest and kept climbing. Getting her hands on the Death Star's plans was one thing. Now they needed to get them into the hands of the Rebel Alliance.

There was no way to get out of the vault the way they'd come. They'd have to find another exit.

As Jyn climbed higher, Cassian shouted out a warning. Three men had appeared in a doorway—an access to the columns inside the data tower. Two of them were death troopers.

Jyn recognized the third from her childhood—from her nightmares.

It was Director Orson Krennic.

CHAPTER 58

BAZE MALBUS had seen enough violence in his time, and he had come to hate it. That was one of the reasons he'd stuck with his friend Chirrut for so long. The monk helped keep him centered, even after he'd lost his own faith in the Force so long before.

Now, though—with Jedha City gone, along with everyone in it he had ever known—Baze had decided to embrace violence once again. He gloried in every stormtrooper he shot dead. Firing a rocket at an AT-ACT thrilled him, even if it hadn't brought the beast down.

Still, the battle rang hollow to him. They weren't trying to destroy the entire facility. They weren't even trying to kill stormtroopers. Their only job was to distract the Imperial forces long enough for Jyn, Cassian, and that turncoat droid of his to get their job done.

Baze wanted to make the Empire hurt. The only chance of doing that was in Jyn's crazy plan, but this battle felt more like a sideshow to him—right up until Bodhi called them for help.

Baze heard the ex-Imperial pilot yelling over Sergeant Melshi's comm. "They've got the plans!" he said. "I'm tied in at my end."

That news lit Baze up. They weren't trying to buy time for a doomed operation any longer. Jyn and Cassian had actually succeeded! Now they just needed to help them get the plans out.

"Rogue One!" Bodhi called. "Can anybody hear me out there? I've got my end tied in! I need an open line!"

Melshi grabbed his comm and shouted into it. "Hang on!" The rebel sergeant turned to Baze. "The master switch! It's out there at that console!"

He pointed to the console station right in front of them. They'd been trying to reach it, but the stormtroopers hadn't given them a centimeter. The air around the thing sang with blaster fire, and venturing into that would be inviting death.

The highest ranking of the rebel soldiers—Lieutenant Sefla, a man who had impressed Baze with his humility and big heart—charged toward it anyway, in a desperate attempt to do his duty. After only a few steps, incoming blaster fire cut him down.

"Come on!" Bodhi's voice grew more desperate through Melshi's comm. "Come on!"

Melshi wasn't the kind of commander to order someone to do something he wasn't willing to try himself. After Sefla had fallen, no one else stepped forward to take the man's place. It was up to him.

Melshi steeled himself and then dashed out into the open. The other rebel soldiers tried to offer him covering fire. Baze joined in, and Chirrut—who was hunkered nearby—assisted with his lightbow.

Melshi got farther than Sefla, but he still fell short of reaching the master switch.

Baze didn't know what to do. He expected one of the other rebel commandos to give it a try next. Or maybe they should all run at the switch together and hope that one of them managed to get through?

Before he could suggest anything, though, the choice was taken from him.

Chirrut rose to his feet and began chanting. "I am one with the Force, and the Force is with me."

Then he stepped forward and began walking toward the master switch. "I am one with the Force, and the Force is with me."

"Chirrut!" Baze shouted after him. The blind fool was sure to get himself killed!

Chirrut strode forward as if he were crossing the street. As he went, he juked this way and that, dodging incoming fire he couldn't even see. The entire time, he kept chanting his mantra. "I am one with the Force, and the Force is with me."

"Chirrut!" Baze pleaded. "Come back!"

Baze was sure that Chirrut's luck would run out sooner rather than later—well before he reached the master switch—but he kept going. "I am one with the Force, and the Force is with me."

Chirrut reached the console and fumbled around its surface, feeling for that elusive master switch. When he found it, he pressed down hard.

CHAPTER 59

BACK IN his stolen shuttle, a light popped on to tell Bodhi that the comm line to the rebel fleet had been opened. He turned on the radio and tried to speak into it calmly and clearly.

"Okay, okay . . . This is Rogue One calling the rebel fleet."

No one responded, and for a moment Bodhi feared something had gone wrong, perhaps behind his control. Had he forgotten something? Was there a connection he'd failed to make?

Had they done all that for nothing?

He tried again. "This is Rogue One calling any Alliance ships that can hear me! *Is there anybody up there?* This is Rogue One! Come in, over."

The radio crackled back at him, and he heard a gravelly voice. "This is Admiral Raddus! Rogue One, we hear you!"

Bodhi wanted to cry and cheer at the same time. He settled for laughing in relief.

"We have the plans!" he said. "They found the Death Star plans. They have to transmit them from the communications tower. You have to take down the shield gate. It's the only way to get it through!"

"Copy you, Rogue One!"

Bodhi heard the admiral turn and address someone in the background. "Call in a Hammerhead corvette. I have an idea."

Bodhi scanned the sky for some hint of what was happening. He focused on the shield gate, hoping he would see some results from his request.

Moments later, he spotted a bright flash of light near where he knew the shield gate sat in the sky. He recognized it as an explosion. Something that size would tear a hole in the shield for sure, so the signal could finally get through.

Bodhi grinned up at the sky. *"This is for you, Galen!"*

Just then, Bodhi heard something come rattling into the cargo shuttle's cabin. Someone must have gotten into the bay and thrown it in there behind him. He spun around to see what it was, already horrified by what he knew he would find.

Sure enough, he spied a grenade on the floor nearby. He didn't even have time to shout before it went off.

CHAPTER 60

BAZE STARED at his friend Chirrut in horror. The monk may have completed his mission, but he was far from out of trouble. The console where he had pushed the master switch was still in the middle of the fire zone.

"Chirrut!" Baze called. "Come here!"

The monk's luck ran out. He made it only two steps toward Baze before the blast from a grenade blew him off his feet.

"*Chirrut!*"

Heedless of the incoming fire that strafed the open ground, Baze charged forward across the sand. He dropped down next to his fallen friend and found he was not quite dead yet. He took his hand.

"Chirrut, don't go. Don't go. I'm here. . . ."

Chirrut wheezed at his old friend. "It's okay. It's okay." He tried to comfort Baze, even with his final breath. "Look for the Force, and you will always find me. . . ."

With that, Chirrut slumped over and the last of his life left his body behind.

Baze glanced over and saw Rogue One's stolen Imperial cargo shuttle explode in flames.

Had Bodhi gotten his message to the rebel fleet? Had they managed to open a hole in the shield?

Baze decided it didn't matter. The stormtroopers had killed Chirrut, the last person in the galaxy he had ever truly cared about. For that, they were going to pay.

He stood up and began firing at anything wearing Imperial

armor. As he did, he chanted a mantra, one that hadn't crossed his lips for a long time.

"The Force is with me, and I am with the Force."

Rather than running back for cover, Baze marched toward the stormtroopers. With every step he took, he fired at them again and again, unleashing a flurry of furious energy bolts from his souped-up blaster. He didn't intend to go down until he'd run through every bit of ammunition piled in his specialized backpack.

Stormtroopers fell to the left, right, and center. One by one, he brought them to their doom. But there were too many of them, even for a man on a righteous mission. He caught an enemy bolt, and it spun him to the ground.

Baze refused to give in. He gritted his teeth and pushed himself back to his feet, still firing every step of the way. The Force was with him.

As he went, he missed a half-downed death trooper who was hefting a grenade. The man pitched it into the sky, and it came down right next to Baze.

He was too hurt to grab it and throw it back. He couldn't even run from it. There was nothing for him to do but glance back at Chirrut and know the two of them would soon be reunited in the Force.

The last thing he heard was the grenade's boom.

CHAPTER 61

THE MOMENT Jyn saw Krennic, she started climbing away from him and his death troopers, trying to put one of the data columns between them and her. The top of the tower wasn't that far away. She just needed to get there and try to escape.

Cassian, on the other hand, drew his blaster and began firing at their attackers. He managed to shoot down one of the death troopers, but Krennic and the other one fired back at him.

Cassian clung closer to the column, but that didn't give him much cover. He couldn't shoot and climb at the same time, so he kept firing, trying to take out their attackers.

"Keep going!" Cassian shouted after Jyn. "Keep going!"

Jyn climbed faster, reaching for freedom. As she did, she glanced down and saw Cassian take a shot from a blaster rifle that knocked him from the data column. He toppled over, out of sight.

She had no time to mourn him then. She just kept climbing, even after she heard a body smash into the distant floor.

At least she'd put enough of the data column between her and the Imperials. Now she just needed to reach the top.

Soon she could see Scarif's sky through the vents at the top of the tower. They pulsed open and closed like something alive, pulling the hot air from the tower and helping preserve the tapes.

The valves, of course, were not designed as doors. To get past them, Jyn would have to leap through at just the right moment. Tired as she was, she worried that she might time her jump badly and be caught inside a valve. She concentrated on the one in front of her and watched it go through a few cycles until she got the rhythm of it down.

Then she made her move.

Once through, Jyn found her way to the top of the tower. She emerged countless stories in the air, with TIE fighters and strikers and rebel X-wings dogfighting in the sky around her. She had walked into the middle of a war.

Somewhere atop the tower, she knew, sat a dish control unit the Empire used to transmit data to ships hovering overhead. If she could find it and slap the tape into it, she could use it to transmit the plans to the rebel fleet.

She spotted the control unit at one end of the tower's roof and headed toward it. Once she got there, she shoved the tape home.

The screen on the control unit started to flash, and a computerized voice began chanting an error message: "*Reset antennae alignment. Reset antennae alignment. Reset antennae alignment.*"

She hadn't gone this far to stop now. She peered down at the screen. The diagram showed that she had to go to the end of a long, thin gantry that stabbed out from the side of the tower's roof.

On a good day, she wouldn't have wanted to be forced to navigate such a rickety structure. With the battle raging around her, she just wanted to find an elevator to take her straight back down to the ground level, where—if she was lucky—the Empire might toss her in a cozy cell.

She didn't hesitate for an instant, though, charging straight ahead.

Her father had died trying to stop the Death Star. The way the battle was going, the others were probably gone, too. Baze, Chirrut, Bodhi, K-2SO—even Cassian. She was the only one left, and she couldn't let their sacrifices be for nothing.

When Jyn reached the end of the gantry, she found a set of controls and turned the knob that would adjust the dish. The computer responded to her again. This time it said, *"Dish aligning. Dish aligning."*

Jyn craned her neck to look up and see the gigantic satellite dish atop the tower moving. It cranked itself back until it was pointing straight up, right toward the shield gate.

"Dish aligned," the computer reported. *"Ready to transmit."*

Jyn wanted to pump her fist in triumph, but her work wasn't done. The channel to the rebel fleet might finally be open, but she still needed to get back to the transmitter and push the button to send the plans.

At that moment, a TIE fighter pilot spotted her standing there, vulnerable and alone, and it screamed straight for her, firing its weapons the entire way. She spun about and charged back down the gantry toward the tower's roof.

She managed to evade the TIE fighter's strike, but the blasts tore the gantry apart. She felt herself falling and reached out to find something—anything—to keep her from toppling off the tower to the ground far below.

CHAPTER 62

GRAND MOFF TARKIN frowned as the Death Star appeared in the sky over Scarif. The rebel fleet had done far more harm to the Star Destroyers than he would have thought possible. Just another example of the incompetence of the managers there, including—especially—Director Krennic.

This would not do.

General Romodi looked at Tarkin from his spot on the bridge. "Sir, shall I begin targeting their fleet?"

It was a fair question, but it showed the same problem in thinking that had allowed the rebels to do so much damage already that day. Tarkin gave the general a shake of his head.

"Lord Vader will handle the fleet. The plans must not be allowed to leave Scarif—at any cost."

It was then that the general understood exactly what Tarkin meant. While the Death Star certainly could take out the entire rebel fleet, doing so would require time. Every moment that slipped past was another moment something could go wrong—something in the rebels' favor.

Vader would be there shortly, and he and his personal Star Destroyer should be more than enough to sweep up the remains of the rebel fleet. That would put an end to the sharp end of the Alliance for good.

Meanwhile, Tarkin would put the Death Star to better use by employing it for its stated purpose. He gazed down at

Scarif. Such a beautiful place, and he would be among the last to see it.

"You may fire when ready," he informed Romodi.

The general immediately set to carrying out his world-ending orders.

CHAPTER 63

SMOKE ROSE from the top of the tower where the TIE fighter's blasts had landed. Satisfied with a job well done, the TIE fighter pilot veered away from the tower and went hunting for fresh targets.

A moment later, Jyn emerged from the smoke, still holding on to the damaged gantry, lucky to be alive. She struggled up the remainder of the gantry until she reached the tower's roof again. As she did, she saw the Death Star appear in the sky.

It loomed over the planet, larger than any moon, and Jyn was under no illusion about what its arrival meant. She'd seen what it and the people in charge of it had done to Jedha City.

Scarif and everyone on it were doomed.

Jyn pulled herself onto the roof. As she did, Director Krennic emerged from a column of smoke in front of her.

She recoiled for an instant as she wondered what to do. When the man came at her with his blaster, though, she knew she couldn't show him an instant of hesitation.

Krennic peered at her, trying to understand the role the young woman before him played in the disaster unfolding around him. "Who *are* you?" he asked.

It had been a long time, and Jyn had only been a little girl the last time the two had met. She remembered him well, despite that.

"You know who I am," she told him. "I'm Jyn Erso. Daughter of Galen and Lyra."

Krennic blinked as he struggled to process that revelation. The girl he'd failed to find on Lah'mu all those years before.

Jyn couldn't let the man believe he'd won. She might not have been able to send the Death Star's plans to the rebel fleet yet, but *he* didn't know that.

"You've lost," she said with as much confidence as she could manage.

"Oh, I have, have I?" It would take more than her word to convince a man as arrogant as Krennic.

"My father's revenge." Jyn let that land, and she savored the look on Krennic's face. "He built a flaw in the Death Star. He put a fuse in the middle of your machine, and I've just told the entire galaxy how to light it."

Krennic shook his head. "The shield is up. Your signal will never reach the rebel base." He leveled his blaster at her. "I've lost nothing but time. You, on the other hand, will die with the Rebellion."

Jyn braced herself for the shot. She was ready to die, but like this? At the hands of the man who'd killed her mother and stolen her father away? And without actually transmitting the plans?

A shot rang out, and for a moment Jyn couldn't understand why she hadn't fallen over in pain. Then Krennic collapsed instead.

She looked beyond the Imperial and saw Cassian standing there, his blaster in hand.

She was thrilled to see that Cassian had survived the fall from the data tower. He must have caught himself before he hit the floor. She wanted to tell him how relieved she was, but she had a job to finish first.

Jyn ran for the control console, grabbed the transmission lever, and hauled it down. The screen began to fill with the data it was preparing to send out. *"Transmitting,"* it said.

They'd done it! Jyn looked to Cassian and gave him the biggest smile she could manage.

She went to his side and put his arm around her shoulders. He could barely walk, but together they made it to the elevator Krennic had taken to the top of the tower.

"You think . . . anybody's listening?" Cassian asked.

"I do." She looked into the sky. "Someone's out there. . . ."

CHAPTER 64

FAR ABOVE, near the shield gate, a communications computer made an announcement to the lieutenant who had been monitoring it. *"Transmissions received."*

The lieutenant turned to shout a report to the rebel cruiser's commander. "Admiral, we have the plans!"

"She did it!" Admiral Raddus said.

He was thrilled. Their desperate gamble—the only shot they had left—had paid off.

Unfortunately, it had come through so late there wasn't anything he could do for the brave people who had stolen the plans for him. As he watched, the dish array on the Death Star charged up. Green lights flashed all around the rim.

The lights became lasers that fired off together. The thin beams coalesced into a single, massive beam of ultimate destruction aimed straight at the planet.

The blast blew through the shield and began cutting into the planet. Raddus and the rest of the rebel fleet still outside the shield could do nothing but gape at it in horror.

"Rogue One," he said. "May the Force be with you."

Then he turned to his bridge crew and began barking out orders. "All ships, prepare for jump to hyperspace!"

Some of the ships managed to get away in no time at all. They must have already planned their escape before they'd gotten their orders. But before they could all get clear, a new ship arrived on the scene.

Raddus recognized it instantly. It was the Star Destroyer

assigned to the Emperor's right hand, the Sith Lord known as Darth Vader.

It opened fire immediately. The barrage of fresh blasts slammed into Raddus's ship, rocking it all the way to the bridge.

Raddus called for a damage report, but he didn't need one. The ship's engines had been disabled, and its hyperspace drive had been knocked offline. They weren't going anywhere.

As Vader's Star Destroyer loomed ever closer, Raddus cast about for a way to get the Death Star plans off his ship and back to Yavin 4, where the Rebel Alliance could analyze them and find the battle station's weakness.

He might not live to see it happen, but that didn't mean the Rebellion was dead yet.

CHAPTER 65

JYN AND CASSIAN made it down to the ground level of the tower and outside of the building without anyone trying to stop them. The rebel commandos were all dead. Bodhi's stolen cargo shuttle was still burning out on landing pad nine.

Anyone who had survived the battle on the main island had already taken to the skies if they could. There would be no escape for anyone else.

Jyn helped Cassian limp away from the tower and toward an unspoiled stretch of beach. When they reached the shore, his legs finally gave out on him, and he fell to the sand.

Jyn knelt down beside him, and they gave each other weary smiles. Cassian looked out at the water and the wave of destruction heading for them.

"I'm glad you came," Jyn told him.

As they watched the Death Star's massive beam cut toward them, trailing a wake of world-shattering destruction, they held each other's hands. Soon they found themselves embracing as they waited for their end.

"Your father would be proud of you, Jyn," Cassian said.

Those were the exact words she needed to hear at that moment. They'd done what they set out to do, and with luck their efforts would give the Rebellion a chance to take the Empire down.

They couldn't ask for anything more than that—and there was nothing they could do to stop what would happen next.

The green beam fluoresced brighter and brighter as it approached, driving the front edge of a spreading explosion before it. The last thing Jyn saw before the blast enveloped her was the color transforming into a cleansing white.

CHAPTER 66

ABOARD RADDUS'S rebel cruiser, a crewman downloaded the Death Star plans onto a data card, just as Raddus had ordered. He then took the card and sprinted off the bridge on his mission.

The corridors of the ship swam with other crew members on various missions of their own. Darth Vader's Star Destroyer had already pulled alongside their vessel, and it would be only a matter of minutes before the Sith Lord's boarding party arrived on the rebel cruiser.

The crewman ran into a security door that had been locked down prematurely. Normally, he would have tried to go around it, down another path in the ship, but he had already run out of time. He began banging on the door to get his crewmates on the other side to open it, but the controls for the door were jammed.

He grabbed a few people passing by and had them help him try to pry the door open with their hands. People on the other side did the same, working as hard as they could.

The time they wished they still had vanished when Darth Vader entered the corridor.

The crewman heard the Sith Lord's horrible breathing first. He glanced back to see a red lightsaber beam leap from its hilt.

Some of the people with the crewman turned and fired at Vader, but he deflected their shots with his blade. Then he held up his hand, and one of the rebels had his blaster torn from his grip by an unseen force.

The crewman set to the door with terror-fueled strength. It slid to the side, although just a crack.

The crewman took the data card and slid it through the sliver of an opening. Someone on the other side grabbed it, and the crewman could hear the man running for his life. Before the crewman could even turn around, though, something yanked him away from the door.

The man who had taken the data card—Toshma Jefkin—charged through the corridors of the ship until he reached the cruiser's docking bay. There he spotted his goal: an Alderaanian blockade runner called the *Tantive IV*.

The moment Toshma boarded the ship, it zoomed away, leaving the docking bay behind. Out of breath, he handed the data card off to a woman who then took it to the ship's captain, Raymus Antilles.

Captain Antilles was happy to be made the custodian of the card for a moment, but he knew it wasn't ultimately for him. "Make sure you secure the airlock," he barked to his junior officers on the bridge. "And prepare the escape pods."

As his people moved off to fulfill their orders, Raymus approached a young woman dressed in a simple white gown. "Your Highness," he said as he presented her with the data card. "The transmission we received."

Bail Organa's daughter, Princess Leia Organa, turned around to accept the card from the captain. She examined it with a quiet look of raw determination.

"What is it they've sent us?" Raymus asked, unable to suppress his curiosity. What, in other words, had Admiral Raddus ordered them to get to the Alliance high council at all costs?

The princess looked at him. Her dark eyes sparkled as she summed up the contents of the data card in a single word.

"Hope."